PARVANA'S JOURNEY

DEBORAH ELLIS

{ ❋ }{ ❋ }{ ❋ }

Parvana's Journey

A GROUNDWOOD BOOK
DOUGLAS & McINTYRE
TORONTO VANCOUVER BERKELEY

Groundwood Books / Douglas & McIntyre
720 Bathurst Street, Suite 500, Toronto, Ontario M5S 2R4

Distributed in the USA by Publishers Group West
1700 Fourth Street, Berkeley CA 94710

We acknowledge for their financial support of our publishing program the Canada Council for the Arts, the Ontario Arts Council and the Government of Canada through the Book Publishing Industry Development Program (BPIDP).

ONTARIO ARTS COUNCIL
CONSEIL DES ARTS DE L'ONTARIO

National Library of Canada Cataloguing in Publication Data
Ellis, Deborah
Parvana's Journey / Deborah Ellis
Sequel to: The breadwinner.
ISBN 0-88899-514-8 (bound).–ISBN 0-88899-519-9 (pbk.)
1. Women–Afghanistan–Social conditions–Juvenile fiction.
2. Taliban–Juvenile fiction. I. Title.
PS8559.L5494P37 2002   jC813'.54   C2002-902756-X
PZ7

Library of Congress Control Number: 2002106836

Cover illustration by Pascal Milelli
Printed and bound in Canada

To children we force to be braver than they
should have to be

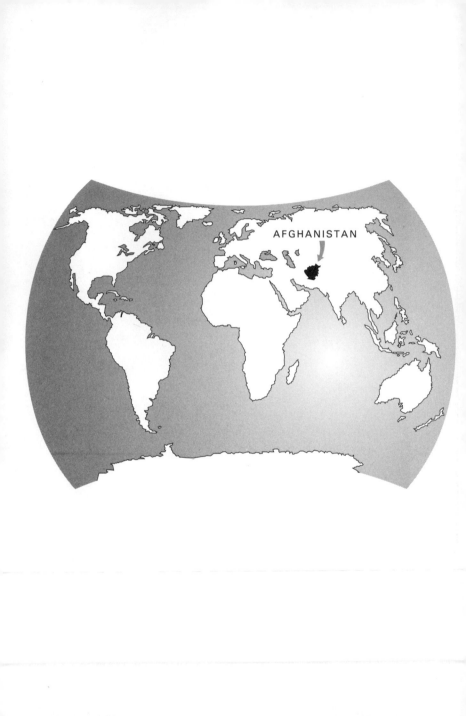

ONE

A man Parvana didn't know gave one final pat to the dirt mounded up over her father's grave. The village mullah had already recited the jenazah, the prayer for the dead. The funeral service was over.

Small, sharp stones dug into Parvana's knees as she knelt at the edge of the grave and placed the large stones she had gathered around it. She put each one down slowly. There was no reason to hurry. She had nowhere else to go.

There were not enough rocks. The ones she had gathered only went halfway around the rectangle of turned-up earth.

"Spread them out," a man said, and he bent down to help her.

They spread out the stones, but Parvana didn't like the gaps. She thought briefly about taking rocks from other graves, but that didn't seem right. She would find more rocks later. One thing Afghanistan had was plenty of rocks.

"Rise yourself up now, boy," one of the men said to her. Parvana's hair was clipped short, and she wore the plain blanket shawl and shalwar kameez of a boy. "There is no point staying in the dirt."

"Leave him alone," another man said. "He is mourning for his father."

"We all have dead to mourn, but we do not have to do it in the dirt. Come on, boy, get to your feet. Be the strong son your father would be proud of."

Go away, Parvana thought. Go away and leave me alone with my father. But she said nothing. She allowed herself to be pulled to her feet. She brushed the dust from her knees and looked around at the graveyard.

It was a large graveyard for such a small village. The graves spread out in a haphazard pattern, as if the villagers thought that each person they buried would be the last.

Parvana remembered digging up bones in a graveyard in Kabul with her friend, Shauzia, to earn money.

I don't want anyone digging up my father, she thought, and she resolved to pile so many rocks on his grave that no one would bother him.

She wanted to tell people about him. That he was a teacher, that he had lost his leg when his school was bombed. That he had loved her and told her stories, and now she was all alone in this big, sad land.

But she kept silent.

The men around her were mostly old. The younger ones were damaged somehow, with an arm missing, or only one eye, or no feet. All the other young men were at war, or dead.

"A lot of people have died here," the man who had helped her said. "Sometimes we are bombed by the Taliban. Sometimes we are bombed by the other side. We used to be farmers. Now we are targets."

Parvana's father hadn't been killed by a bomb. He had just died.

"Who are you with now, boy?"

Parvana's jaw hurt as she held her face tight to keep from crying.

"I am alone," she managed to say.

"You will come home with me. My wife will take care of you."

There were only men at her father's graveside. The women had to stay in their homes. The Taliban didn't like women walking around on their own, but Parvana had given up trying to understand why the Taliban hated women. There were other things to think about.

"Come, boy," the man urged. His voice was kind. Parvana left her father's grave and went with him. The other men followed. She could hear the scuff of their sandals on the hard, dusty ground.

"What is your name?" the man asked.

"Kaseem," Parvana replied, giving him her boy-name. She didn't think any more about whether to trust someone with the truth about herself. The truth could get her arrested, or killed. It was easier and safer not to trust anyone.

"We will go first to your shelter and retrieve your belongings. Then we will go to my home." The man knew where Parvana and her father had set up their lean-to. He had been one of the men who had carried her father's body to the graveyard. Parvana thought he might have been one of the men who had checked in on them regularly, helping with her father's care, but she couldn't be sure. Everything about the past few weeks was blurry in her memory.

The lean-to was on the edge of the village, against a mud wall that had crumbled from a bomb blast. There wasn't much to retrieve. Her father had been buried in all the clothes that he owned.

Parvana crawled into the lean-to and gathered her things together. She wished she could have some privacy, so she could cry and think about her father, but the roof and walls were made of a sheet of clear plastic. She knew the man could see her as he waited patiently for her to go home with him. So she concentrated on the task in front of her and did not allow herself to cry.

She rolled the blankets, her extra shalwar kameez and the little cook-pot into a bundle. This was the same bundle she had carried on their long journey from Kabul. Now she would have to carry the other things, too — her father's shoulder bag where he kept his paper, pens and little things like matches, and the precious bundle of books they'd kept hidden from the Taliban.

She backed out of the lean-to, pulling the bundles out with her. She took the plastic down from where it had been spread over a ragged corner of the building, folded it up and added it to her blankets.

"I'm ready," she said.

The man picked up one of the bundles. "Come with me," he said, leading the way through the village.

Parvana paid no attention to the rough mud-walled houses and piles of bomb-damaged rubble that made up the village. She had seen many places like it, traveling with her father. She no longer tried to imagine what the village might have looked like before it was bombed, with homes in good repair, children playing and flowers blooming. Who had time for flowers now? It was hard enough just finding something to eat every day. She kept her head down and kicked at pebbles as she walked.

"Here is my house." The man stood before a small mud hut. "Five times my house has been destroyed by bombs, and five times I have built it back up again," he said proudly.

A flap of tattered green cloth covered the doorway. He held it aside and motioned for Parvana to go in.

"Here is the grieving boy," he said to his wife. The woman, crouching over her needlework, put aside her sewing and stood up.

Parvana was young, so the woman did not put on her burqa. Three small girls watched from a corner of the room.

As a guest, Parvana was given the best spot in the dark one-room house. She sat on the thickest mat on the floor and drank the tea the man's wife brought her. The tea was weak, but its warmth soothed her.

"We lost our son," the woman said. "He died of a sickness, like two of our daughters. Maybe you could stay here and be our son."

"I have to find my family," Parvana said.

"You have family besides your father?"

"My mother, my older sister, Nooria, my younger sister, Maryam, and my baby brother, Ali." Parvana saw them in her mind as she spoke their names. She wanted to cry again. She wanted to hear her mother tell her to do her chores, or Nooria say something bossy, or feel the little ones' arms around her.

"I have family in many places, too," the woman said. She was about to say more when some neighbor men came into the house. She quickly took her burqa down from a nail, put it over her head and fetched the men some tea. Then she sat in a corner, quiet and faceless.

The men sat on the mats along the walls and looked at Parvana. They had been at the graveside.

"Do you have other family somewhere?" one of them asked.

Parvana repeated their names. It was easier the second time.

"Are they in Pakistan?"

I don't know where they are," Parvana said. "My father and I traveled from Kabul to look for them. They went to Mazar-e-Sharif for my sister's wedding, but the Taliban took over the city, and now I don't know where they are. My father and I spent the winter in a camp north of Kabul. He was ill then, but when spring came, he thought he was well enough to continue."

Parvana did not want to talk about her father's growing weakness. For days, it seemed as though he would die while they walked alone through the Afghan wilderness. When they arrived at the village, he just could not go any farther.

For so long now they had been wandering from village to village, from temporary settlement to larger camps for people displaced by the war. There were times on the journey when his cough and his weariness were so bad he could not leave the lean-to. There was never much food, but sometimes he was even too tired to eat what there was. Parvana would scramble through the camp, desperately searching for things that would tempt her father to eat, but often she would come back to the lean-to empty-handed.

She did not speak to these men of those times. She also did not tell them that her father had been in prison, arrested by the Taliban for being educated in England.

"You can stay here with us in this village," one of the men said. "You can make your home here."

"I have to find my family."

"That is important," one of the men said, "but it is not safe for you to wander around Afghanistan on your own. You will stay here. You can continue your search when you are grown."

Weariness hit Parvana like a tank. "I will stay," she said. Suddenly she was too tired to argue. Her head slouched down on her chest, and she felt the woman in the house lay her down and cover her with a blanket. Then she fell asleep.

Parvana stayed in the village for another week. She piled rocks on her father's grave and tried to become brave enough to leave.

The girls in the family helped her feel better. She played string games with the little ones. The older girl, who seemed only a couple of years younger than Parvana, went with her each day to her father's grave and helped carry and pile the rocks to keep him safe.

It was comforting to have a mother taking care of her again, too, cooking for her and watching out for her, even though it wasn't her own mother. It made her feel almost normal to be around the everyday tasks of ordinary living, the cooking and cleaning. As a guest she was not expected to help, so she spent most of her time resting and mourning her father. She was tempted to stay and be a son to the good people who had taken her in. The journey ahead of her would be long and lonely.

But she had to find the people she belonged to. She could not pass as a boy forever. She was already thirteen.

One afternoon toward the end of the week,

a group of children poked their heads in the door of the house where Parvana was staying.

"Can we take you today?" they asked. "Can you come now?"

The children had been begging for days for her to go with them to see the village's main attraction. Parvana hadn't felt like seeing anything, but today she said, "All right, let's go."

The children pulled her by the hand up a hill on the far side of the village from the graveyard.

A rusty Soviet tank stood on the top of the hill, hidden by some boulders. The children scrambled on it like it was the swing set Parvana dimly remembered from her old schoolyard in Kabul. They played battle, shooting each other with finger-guns until they were all dead, then jumping up to do it all again.

"Isn't this fine?" they asked Parvana. "We are the only village in this area with its own tank."

Parvana agreed the tank was lovely. She didn't tell them that she'd seen many other tanks, and crashed-down war planes, too. She always avoided them, afraid the ghosts of the people who died in them would jump out and grab her.

Parvana was awakened the next night by a gentle shake. A small hand was pressed over her mouth to prevent her from crying out.

"Come outside," a voice whispered in her ear. The oldest girl took up Parvana's bundles and went out the door. They had to be very quiet. The rest of the family was asleep in the room.

Parvana held her sandals and her blanket shawl and crept out of the house.

"You must leave now," the girl said once they were outside. "I heard the old men talking. They are going to turn you over to the Taliban. Some soldiers are coming by here any day, and the men think the Taliban will pay them money for you."

Parvana wrapped her blanket around her shoulders and slipped her feet into her sandals. She was shaking. She knew that what the girl was saying was true. She had heard many stories about this in the winter camp where she and her father had stayed.

"Here is some food and drink," the girl said, handing Parvana a cloth parcel. "It's all I dared to take without being caught. Maybe it will last until you get to the next village."

"How do I thank you?"

"Take me with you," the girl pleaded. "My life here is nothing. There has to be some place better than this on the other side of those hills, but I can't go by myself."

Parvana couldn't look at the girl's face. If she took the girl with her, all the men of the village would come after them. The girl would be in terrible trouble for dishonoring her family, and Parvana would be turned over to the Taliban.

She put her arms around the girl, aching for her sisters.

"Go back inside," she said stiffly. "I can't help you." Then she picked up her belongings, turned quickly and walked out of the village without looking back.

She didn't stop walking until the sun hung low in the sky late the next day. She found a spot sheltered from the wind by some boulders and gazed out at the magnificent Afghan landscape. The land was bare and rocky, but the hills picked up the color of the sky and now glowed a brilliant red.

She sat down and ate some nan and drank cold tea. There was not another person in sight, just hills and sky.

"I'm all alone," she said out loud. Her words drifted away into the air.

She wished she had someone to talk to.

"I wish Shauzia were here," she said. Shauzia was her best friend. They had pretended to be boys together in Kabul so they could earn money. But Shauzia was somewhere in Pakistan. There was no way to talk to her.

Or maybe there was. Parvana reached into her father's shoulder bag — her shoulder bag now — and took out a pen and a notebook. Using the surface of the bag as a desk, she began to write.

Dear Shauzia:
A week ago, I buried my father...

TWO

"Fourteen times five is seventy. Fourteen times six is eighty-four. Fourteen times seven is ninety-eight." Parvana recited the multiplication tables to herself as she walked over the barren hills. Her father had got her into the habit.

"The world is our classroom," he always said, before giving Parvana a science or a geography lesson. He had been a history teacher, but he knew a lot about other subjects, too.

Sometimes they were able to ride in the back of a cart or a truck from village to village or from camp to camp as they searched for the rest of the family. Often, though, they had to walk, and the lessons made the journey go by more quickly.

If they were alone, he taught her to speak and read English, scratching letters into the dirt when they stopped for a rest. He told her stories from Shakespeare's plays and talked about England, where he had gone to university.

On clear nights, if he wasn't too tired, he taught her about the stars and the planets. During the long, cold winter months, he told her about the great Afghan and Persian poets. He would recite their poems, and she would repeat them over and over until she knew them by heart.

"Your brain needs exercise, just like your body," he said. "A lazy brain does no one any good."

Sometimes they talked about the family as they walked along. "How big is Ali now?" her father would ask. He had been in jail for many months, and by the time he was released, the little boy had left Kabul with the rest of the family. Parvana would try to remember how big her brother was the last time she'd held him, and then they would imagine how much he might have grown since then.

"Maryam is very smart," Parvana would remember.

"All my girls are smart," her father would say. "You will all grow into strong, brave women and you will rebuild our poor Afghanistan."

Whenever Parvana and her father talked

about the family, it was as though Mother and the children were just off on a holiday, safe and happy. They never spoke about their worries.

Sometimes they walked in silence. Those were the times when her father was in too much pain to talk. The injuries he had suffered when his school was bombed had never completely healed. The beatings in prison and the bad food and poor medical care in the camps meant that he was often in pain.

Parvana hated those times, when there was nothing she could do to make anything better.

"We can stop for awhile, Father," she would say.

"If we stop, we die," her father always replied. "We will go on."

Parvana's belly had a familiar ache today. The small bit of cooked rice, nan and dried mulberries given to her by the village girl had lasted three days. She would eat only small portions at each meal, then tie up the food again quickly in its cloth bundle so she wouldn't gulp it all at once. But it had been four days since she left the village, and now everything was gone.

"Fourteen times eight is one hundred and

twelve. Fourteen times nine is one hundred and twenty-two...no, that's not right." She tried to figure out her mistake, but she was too hungry to think properly.

A sound reached Parvana's ears across the empty stretch of land — a sound not human, not animal, and not machine. It rose and fell, and for awhile Parvana thought it was the wind whining around the hills. But the day was still. Not even a breeze played around her neck.

Parvana walked through a small valley with not-too-tall hills all around her. The strange sound bounced from hill to hill. She couldn't be sure where it was coming from. She thought about hiding, but there were no trees or boulders to crouch behind.

"I'll just keep going," she said out loud, and the sound of her own voice gave her some small comfort.

She turned down a bend in the valley trail, and the sound came at her in a rush.

It was coming from right above her.

Parvana looked up and saw the crouched figure of a woman sitting on the top of the little hill. Her burqa had been flung back, and her face was showing. The unearthly noise was coming from her.

Parvana trudged up the hill. The climb was hard with the load on her back, and she was sweating and breathing hard by the time she got to the top.

Catching her breath before she spoke, Parvana stood in front of the woman and gave her a little wave.

The wailing did not stop.

"Are you all right?" Parvana asked. There was no response. "Do you have anything to eat or drink?" Still nothing but wailing.

Where could the woman have come from? Parvana could see no village or settlement nearby. The woman had no bags or bundles with her — nothing to show she was on any sort of journey.

"What's your name?" Parvana asked. "Where do you come from? Where are you going?" The woman didn't look at her or show any sign at all that she knew Parvana was standing in front of her.

Parvana dropped her bundles and waved her arms in front of the woman's face. She jumped up and down and clapped her hands right beside the woman's ear. Still nothing but wailing.

"Stop that noise!" Parvana shouted. "Stop it! Pay attention to me!" She bent down and grabbed the woman by the shoulders and shook her roughly. "You're a grownup! You have to take care of me!"

Still the woman kept wailing.

Parvana wanted to strike her. She wanted to kick her and shove her until the woman shut up and fed her. She was shaking with fury and actually raised a hand to slap her when she took a closer look at the woman's eyes.

The eyes were dead. There was no life left in them. Parvana had seen that look before, in the camp for internal refugees. She had seen people who had lost everything and had given up hope that they would ever have love or tenderness or laughter again.

"Some people are dead before they die," her father once told her. "They need quiet, rest, a special doctor who knows of such things, and a glimpse of something better down the road. But where will they find these things in this camp? It is hard enough to find a blanket. Avoid these people, Parvana. You cannot help them, and they will take away your hope."

Parvana remembered her father's words. She no longer felt like hitting the woman. Since the woman could not help her, and she could not help the woman, Parvana picked up her bundles and went back down the hill. Then she walked quickly away until she had left the sound of the woman's grief far, far behind.

THREE

L ater that afternoon, Parvana lay on her belly at the top of a small ridge, peering into the clearing below.

A small group of mud huts — a tiny village — was in ruins. Parvana recognized the sort of damage that came from bombs. There had been a war going on in Afghanistan for more than twenty years. Someone was always bombing someone else. Lots of bombs had fallen on Kabul. Bombs had fallen everywhere.

Nothing was moving below except for a piece of cloth fluttering in a doorway.

Parvana knew that sometimes soldiers would move into a village after bombing it and live in the houses people had abandoned. She had seen them do this in her travels with her father.

She watched the village for a long time but saw no other movement. Slowly she went down the hill. Much of the wall around the village had been destroyed, but there were still many places where soldiers could be hiding.

Parvana walked into the little settlement, stepping carefully through the rubble. She peered into what was left of the one-room houses. Mattresses, rugs, cook-pots and tea cups were scattered everywhere.

She recognized the look. It was the run-for-your-life look. She had seen her own houses look like this as her family grabbed a few possessions and ran out just ahead of the bombs.

She wondered where the people from these houses had gone. They would probably come back to rebuild when they thought it was safe.

It was eerie standing by herself in the deserted village. She felt as though she were being watched, but there was no one left to see.

A thin wail drifted on the breeze. It sounded like a kitten. Parvana followed the sound.

The cry came from the last house. Parvana stood at the doorway. Part of the ceiling had fallen in, and she looked over the rubble for the source of the sound.

Then she saw it. It wasn't a kitten.

In a corner of the room was a baby, lying on its back. A piece of dirty cloth barely covered it, as if it had been blown there by the wind. The baby cried without energy. It cried as if it had been crying for a long time and no longer expected anyone to come.

Parvana went to it.

"Did they leave you all alone? Come on, you poor thing." She lifted the little creature into her arms. "Did your people get scared and forget about you?"

Then she heard the flies and saw the dead woman crushed under the rubble.

Parvana quickly took the child outside, shading its eyes from the bright sun.

"You weren't forgotten," she said. "Your mother would have taken you if she could."

In the light, Parvana could see that the child was a boy, half naked and filthy.

"We'll have to get you clean," she said. "But first we'll feed you. There must be some food around here somewhere."

Parvana took the baby to the least damaged of the houses. She tried to put him down so she could search for things he needed, but the child clung to her and screeched. He wasn't about to be left alone again!

"It's all right, baby. I won't leave you." She

put her father's books and her other things down instead.

The house she was in only had one room. In a corner was a pot with some rice in it. The rice was moldy, but she could scrape off the mold. There was also a small pile of nan, very hard and stale, but what did that matter? It was food.

"We'll have a feast, baby," Parvana said. She had noticed a stream at the edge of the village. She took a pot off the shelf in the house and went to fetch water.

The baby wasn't very good at drinking from a cup. Most of the water went down his front, but Parvana was sure he must have swallowed some. She soaked some stale nan in a bit of water and fed that to the baby, too. He ate everything she gave him, keeping his eyes locked onto hers.

"You're the size my brother Ali was when I last saw him," she said. "No, I'm wrong. You're smaller. Anyway, I know all about the messes babies make. I'll get you clean, and then I'll get myself clean. Then we'll have some more to eat."

She had to go back into the baby's house to

see whether there were any clean clothes for him. She found a little knitted suit, some cloths to use for diapers and a little hat for his head. The house was too damaged to hunt for more things, and Parvana didn't like being around the body of the baby's mother.

I should bury her, Parvana thought, but I can't. I just can't.

She tossed a bit of cloth over the woman's face, which might at least keep the flies away. She didn't want to have to come back here again.

Then she took the baby and the clean clothes down to the stream.

"You're such a good boy," she said as she took off his filthy clothes and washed him. She used the silly sing-song voice that people used to talk to babies. "You'll be easy to take care of. No trouble at all. It will be like having a puppy." Parvana had always wanted a puppy.

The water was cold, but the little boy didn't complain. He just kept looking at Parvana. There was a rash on his body from being in dirty diapers for so long, and he was very thin, but otherwise he seemed unhurt.

Parvana dressed him in clean clothes.

"Doesn't that feel better?"

Parvana didn't know whether the boy's family had spoken Dari or not. Maybe they were Pashtun speakers, and he didn't understand a word she was saying. She decided it didn't matter. It was just nice to have someone to talk to.

She propped the baby up between some rocks with a blanket behind him for padding, so he could see that she wasn't going away. Laying her spare shalwar kameez close by, she took off her own filthy clothes and jumped into the water.

"Yes, I know I'm a girl," she said to the baby. "But that will be our secret, all right?" The baby gurgled.

She used sand to scrub the grime off her skin and clothes, which she spread in the sun to dry.

Back in the least damaged house, she shared some more stale bread with the baby. With a full belly, the little boy fell asleep.

Parvana gently put him down on a toshak and covered him up. She sat down beside him and watched him sleep. He was clean and beautiful, and when she touched his little palm, his tiny fingers curled around her bigger one. She could see no war in his sleeping face, or in the way his breathing made his little chest rise and fall.

"I'll call you Hassan," she said, "because everybody has to have a name."

She stretched out beside him. "Pleasant dreams," she whispered. Then she fell asleep herself.

Parvana stretched herself awake the next morning, enjoying the softness of the mattress underneath her. She usually slept on the hard ground. Sleepily, she wondered whether she could roll the mattress into a small enough bundle to carry with her.

Hassan made a noise, and Parvana became fully awake. He was watching her, and when he saw that she saw him, he gave her a goofy little grin and waved his arms around.

"Good morning, Hassan," Parvana said. It was wonderful to have company.

She picked him up and carefully looked outside. Everything was quiet. No army had come into the village while they had been sleeping.

"Are you hungry, Hassan?" she asked. "How about some golden rice pilaf, with extra raisins, and huge chunks of roasted lamb buried in it? Then we'll have some bolani dumplings, and some tomatoes and onions, and lots of sweet noodle pudding. Doesn't that sound good?"

While she described the menu, Parvana settled Hassan onto her hip. He clung there like a monkey she had once seen in her school geography book clutching a tree branch. She scraped the fuzzy green mold off the cold rice in the pot and shared it with him.

After breakfast, they explored the rest of the little settlement for things they could use. Parvana stayed away from the baby's house, and they saw no more bodies.

A tiny building behind the houses turned out to be a small barn with two goats and a few chickens. Parvana had a vague idea how to milk a goat, and she was thrilled when all her squeezing actually resulted in milk spurting into a bowl. She gave a lot of it to Hassan and drank some herself. It was warm and sweet.

The hens didn't want her taking their eggs, and they kept pecking at her hands whenever she got close to them.

"I need those eggs more than you do," she said, finally picking up a bit of old board and swatting at the chickens until they hopped out of their nests, squawking with annoyance. She put the eggs high on a shelf in the house where she slept. She didn't want to step on them by accident.

As long as Hassan could see her, he didn't fuss, so Parvana made sure they were always close together.

She went from house to house, pulling out of the rubble anything that could still be used. She put everything on a long piece of plastic sheeting and dragged it from house to house. When she was finished, everything was spread out before her.

"I don't like taking other people's things," she said to Hassan, "but if I'm going to take care of you, your village will have to help me."

Parvana looked at everything she had scavenged and carefully chose what she could carry with her. She already had a small cook-pot, but she did take a sharp knife, an extra blanket, some candles, a few boxes of matches, a small pair of scissors and a length of rope. She added a long-handled spoon and two drinking cups. The cups were small, and maybe she could teach Hassan to hold one. He looked smart enough.

She made a food bundle, too, with flour, rice, onions, carrots and some dried apricots — all the food she could find. She put a small tin jug of cooking oil into the bundle.

Finally she added a wonderful find — a bar of soap wrapped in paper with roses on it. The wrapping looked old. Parvana wondered where the people had got it and what special occasion they were saving it for.

She placed both bundles by the door of the least-damaged house, next to her other belongings.

"Now we're ready to continue our journey," she said to Hassan. "We're going to find my mother. I'll let her help me take care of you, but I'm going to be your boss, not her, all right? Nooria — that's my older sister — will definitely try to boss you. She can't help it. She's naturally bossy. But I won't let her."

She was ready to leave but didn't want to.

"I'll just tidy up the house first," she said to Hassan, who was watching her sleepily from the toshak.

With a small whisk broom she found hanging on a nail, Parvana gave the floor a good sweeping. There was a lot of dust, and it took her a long time, but the floor looked better when she was finished. The rest of the little house looked dusty now compared to the clean floor, so she left Hassan sleeping on the mattress and ran down to the stream to fill a pot with water. She wiped down all the walls and shelves, going back to the stream twice for clean water. The whole house soon looked much better.

"I could plant some rose bushes outside," she said quietly, so as not to wake the baby. Afghanistan used to have beautiful gardens. She'd heard about them from her parents. The gardens had all been destroyed by bombs before she was born.

She emptied the dusty water outside the door of the house, spread out her cleaning cloth to dry, and realized that she was very tired. She stretched out beside Hassan and soon fell asleep.

She woke up in the middle of the night. Everything was dark, and for a moment she couldn't remember where she was. She began to panic. Then Hassan moved a bit in his sleep. She curled around him, closed her eyes to keep the darkness out, and fell back asleep.

She built a cook fire the next morning down by the stream and decided to fry all five of the eggs she'd found. Too late, she realized she should have put some oil in the cook-pot, because the eggs stuck to the bottom and didn't hold their shape the way fried eggs did when her mother made them. Still, they tasted very good, and she and Hassan ate every scrap. She even scraped the bottom of the pot with a stick to get the last bits.

Eggs made Parvana think of chickens.

"How hard can it be to kill a chicken?" she asked Hassan.

She carried him to the little barn and they drank more fresh goat's milk. Then she propped the baby up against some straw and turned her attention to the chickens.

"One of you is going to be our dinner," she announced. "Any volunteers?"

No chicken stepped forward.

"I'm bigger than you are," she reminded them, turning toward the fattest one. It stared back at her as she crept closer and closer. Then, just as she was about to grab it, it flew out of her way.

Hassan laughed.

"You're not helping," Parvana said, but she was laughing, too.

None of the chickens felt like being caught, and they made Parvana chase them all over the little barn, to Hassan's great delight.

She was just getting ready to make a final great leap on a chicken she had cornered, when something outside the barn window caught her eye.

In the next instant she had grabbed Hassan and was running madly back to the house where they had slept. She scooped up their bundles of belongings and ran in a panic out of the village.

She had seen, in the distance, the black turbans of Taliban soldiers. They were heading toward her village. If they found her and thought she was a boy, they might force her into their army. If they found her and discovered she was a girl...

That was too horrible to think about.

Parvana didn't think. She just ran, up and over the hill away from the village.

Why Hassan didn't cry out, why the Taliban didn't see her scurrying over the hill, why she didn't stumble under the weight of all she carried, Parvana never knew. She ran and kept running. When she finally stopped, there were three hills between her and the Taliban.

Hassan wasn't at all disturbed at being jostled about. He thought it was great fun and gave her a big grin.

"It must be nice to be young," Parvana said, catching her breath and wiping the drool from Hassan's face.

She knew she could not keep carrying everything. The weight of her bundle would wear her out before she got anywhere. But she dared not get rid of any food.

"We don't know when we'll get more," she said to Hassan.

She opened the other bundles and decided they would probably need everything in them, as well.

That left her father's books.

She opened up that bundle. Four big books with thick hard covers and one small book with a paper cover lay on the cloth. There was also a copy of the secret women's magazine her mother had written articles for back in Kabul. It had been smuggled into Afghanistan by women who had printed it in Pakistan. Parvana was supposed to give it to her mother when they saw each other again.

"I'll bury the biggest three books," she said, "and come back some day and dig them up again."

Using a rock to help her dig through the hard ground, she made a hole big enough for the books. One book was about science, one was about history, and the third was a book of Persian poetry. She couldn't spare a cloth to wrap them in, so the red dirt was plopped right on top of the covers.

She patted down the soil, then kicked some rocks and pebbles on top so no one would be able to tell something was buried there. She thought of her father being underground with his books. Now he would have something to read.

With a heavy heart, Parvana picked up her bundles and the baby, and walked on.

FOUR

Crouching near the mouth of the cave, Parvana listened for the sounds of something that might have gone in there before her.

Hassan fussed and wriggled. Parvana put a finger over his lips, but he either didn't understand or he didn't care. He kept whining and kicking and making screechy little baby noises.

Carrying a baby on a journey was different from carrying a bundle. A bundle could be tossed over one shoulder or the other. A bundle could be dropped when her arms were tired, or even thrown to the ground when she was frustrated and didn't know which way to go next.

But a baby had to be carried carefully and couldn't be dropped, tossed or thrown. Hassan was cute, but he could also be heavy and cranky and smelly to carry.

Parvana's back and shoulders ached. There was no comfortable way to carry everything she needed, and not even multiplication tables took away the pain.

The cave, by a small stream, would be a good place to rest for a few days, as long as there were no wolves inside.

Hassan let out a big squeal, and Parvana gave up any hope of trying to sneak in. She walked up to the entrance and peered in, then stepped inside.

The cave was more of a low-hanging rock than a real cave. As her eyes began to get used to the dimmer light, she could see bits of the back wall. The cave was tall enough for her to stand up in and wide enough for her to stretch out, with plenty of room left over for her bundles. The rocks rose up around it like a cocoon, creating a cozy shelter where she could sleep safely without the risk of anyone creeping up on her. She would stay here for awhile and rest her arms.

"Get out of my cave!"

Parvana spun around and was running away before the voice stopped echoing off the cave walls. Fear kept her legs moving long after she was exhausted.

When she finally slowed down, her brain

began to tell her something she had been too scared to hear moments earlier.

The voice that had yelled at her from the back of the cave was a child's voice.

Parvana stopped running and caught her breath. She turned around and looked back at the cave. She wasn't going to let some child keep her from getting a few days of rest!

"Let's go and see who's in there," she said to Hassan.

She went back to the mouth of the cave.

"Hello," she called in.

"I told you to get out of my cave!" the voice shouted. It was definitely a child's voice.

"How do I know it's your cave?" Parvana asked.

"I've got a gun. Go away or I'll shoot you."

Parvana hesitated. Lots of young boys in Afghanistan did have guns. But if he had a gun, why hadn't he shot at her already?

"I don't believe you," Parvana said. "I don't think you're a killer. I think you're a kid just like me."

She took a few more steps forward, trying to see in the dark.

A stone hit her on the shoulder.

"Stop that!" she shouted. "I'm carrying a baby."

"I warned you to stay away."

"All right, you win," Parvana said. "Hassan and I will leave you alone. We just thought you'd like to share our meal, but I guess you'd rather throw stones."

There was a moment's silence.

"Leave the food and go."

"I have to cook it first," Parvana said over her shoulder as she walked away. "If you want it, come out and get it."

Parvana put down the baby where she could watch him and kept talking while she gathered dried grasses and stalks from dead weeds for a cook fire. The water in the stream was clear and moving swiftly, so she thought it would be safe to drink without boiling it first.

She dipped in her pan. "Here's some lovely cool water to drink, Hassan," she said. "Tastes good, doesn't it? Drink it all down, and we'll have a hot tasty supper." She gave him a piece of stale nan to keep him quiet until the meal was ready.

Parvana heard a little shuffling noise. Out of the corner of her eye she saw a small boy peering out from the cave. He was sitting on the ground. She took him some water.

Dirt covered every inch of him, and he stank like the open sewers that ran through the camp where she had spent the winter. One of his pant legs lay flat against the ground, empty where his leg should have been. He was, Parvana thought, nine or ten years old.

She put the water down where he could reach it, then went back to her work. She heard him gulping the water.

"Bring me some food," the boy ordered, tossing the pot at her.

"I don't like having things thrown at me," Parvana said. "If you want food, come and get it yourself."

"I can't walk!" he yelled. "How stupid you are, not to notice that. Now bring me some food!"

Parvana walked over with some stale nan. The boy glowered at her with hatred and rage. And fear, she thought. His hair was matted with dirt. His face was scratched and his clothes were torn. She kept the bread out of his reach.

"Have you really got a gun?" she asked.

"I'm not telling you." He reached for the bread.

"You give me an answer and I'll give you some food."

The boy flew into a furious burst of temper. He cursed and yelled and threw fistfuls of rocks and dust at Parvana. The fit left him panting and coughing. His cough was deep and used up his whole chest, just like her father's cough had done. Parvana wondered how someone so scrawny found the strength to be so unpleasant.

I could blow on him and he'd fall over, she thought.

"No, I don't have a gun," the boy finally admitted, "but I can get one any time I want, so just watch what you do!"

Parvana gave him the bread. It disappeared in a flash. She fetched more water and put it to boil over the little fire. When the rice was cooked, she put some on a flat rock and took it to the boy.

"What's your name?"

The boy frowned and stared at the rice. "Asif." Parvana gave him the rice. Then she fed Hassan.

"My name is Parvana," she said, putting fingerfuls of rice into Hassan's mouth. "I'm looking for my family. I found this baby in a village that had been bombed. I call him Hassan." She ate some rice herself.

"Why do you have a girl's name?" Asif asked.

Parvana turned suddenly cold. How could she have made such a mistake? Quickly she tried to think of something to say to cover up, but she was suddenly too tired to lie.

"I am a girl," she said. "I pretended to be a boy in Kabul so I could work. When my father and I started out on this journey, it was easier to keep pretending to be a boy."

"Why didn't your father work? Was he lazy?"

"No, my father was not lazy, and don't you dare say another word about him!" Parvana slammed the ground with a rock. The noise startled Hassan and made him cry.

"I'll say what I please. I don't take orders from a girl," Asif taunted.

"You'll take orders from me if you want to eat any more of my food," Parvana yelled. "Oh, be quiet, Hassan!"

Yelling at the baby to stop crying only made him cry louder and longer.

Parvana turned her back on both of them. She tried to ignore them as she watched the flames of her smoky little fire dwindle into embers.

Finally she was calm. Hassan's cry had faded to a thin whimper. Parvana picked him up and held him in her lap until he fell asleep. Then she spread out a blanket and wrapped him up against the night chill.

She had almost forgotten about the cave boy, when he asked her another question.

"So where is your father now?"

Parvana put a few stray strands of camel-grass on the coals and watched as they burst into quick flames.

"He's dead," she answered quietly.

Asif was silent again for awhile. Then he said, "I knew you were a girl. You're far too ugly to be a boy." His voice was weaker than before, as though all the fight had been drained out of him. Parvana saw that he was lying down. She took him a blanket.

"What were you doing in that cave?"

"I'm not answering any more of your stupid questions."

"Tell me, and I'll let you use this blanket."

"I don't want your stinking blanket," he replied, mumbling into the dirt. Parvana wasn't sure whether to kick him or cover him.

Then Asif spoke again, so quietly that she had to lean down to hear him.

"I was chased into the cave by a monster," he said. "I mean, I was chasing a monster. It disappeared into a hole in the cave, and it will probably come out tonight and gobble you up, which will make me very happy."

Parvana walked away without kicking him or covering him. She left the blanket on the ground just out of his reach.

She sat down beside Hassan. There was a tiny bit of light left in the sky. She took out her notebook and pen.

Dear Shauzia:

I met a strange creature today. He's part boy and part wild animal. One of his legs is missing, and he's been hiding in a cave.

You'd think he'd be grateful to me for taking care of him, but he just gets ruder and ruder. How can someone that small be so awful?

Doesn't matter. He's not my problem. In the morning I'll leave him behind. I've got to find my family, and he will just slow me down.

Maybe I should leave the baby behind, too. These boys are not my brothers. They are not my problem.

The evening was too dark to write any more. Parvana put her writing things away. She looked up at the sky for awhile, remembering her father's astronomy lessons.

She got to her feet again and walked back to Asif. He was sleeping flat against the earth, almost hugging the hard ground. She picked up the nearby blanket. She covered him up, then went to sleep beside Hassan.

FIVE

"You need a bath," Parvana said to Asif. "Don't tell me what to do," Asif snapped.

"You stink."

"So do you."

"No, I don't," Parvana said, although she probably did, at least a little. Not as bad as Asif, though.

"If you don't wash, you don't eat," she declared.

"I don't need your lousy food. I've got lots of food in the cave. Good food, too. Not the swill you cook."

"All right, rot away in your stink. I don't care. We're leaving you today anyway, although we'll have to walk miles and miles to get away from your smell. We'll probably have to walk all the way to France."

"France? There's no such place as France."

"You've never heard of France? And you call *me* stupid?"

Asif threw the blanket at her. It didn't go very far, because in mid-throw he started coughing. His shirt was ripped in the middle, and Parvana could see his ribs straining with the effort of trying to breathe between coughs.

She spun on her heels and snapped the blanket in the air to shake the dirt out of it. The dust made her sneeze, which only made her more angry.

"You made my blanket stink," she accused Asif, who was too busy coughing to take any notice of her. She spread the blanket out in the sun to make it smell better. It was something her father had taught her.

"You stink, too," she snarled at Hassan. At least there was someone who had to do what she said. She snatched him away from the stones he was happily bumping together and began undressing him roughly.

Hassan screamed with rage.

"You're doing that all wrong."

Parvana jumped at the suddenness of Asif's voice and turned to see that he had slithered over to the stream on his backside.

"How dare you sneak up on me!"

"You're doing that all wrong," he said again.

"I know exactly what I'm doing. I have a younger brother and sister."

"They must hate you."

"They love me. I'm the best big sister in the whole world."

"They're probably jumping for joy that you're lost out here, because they'll never have to see you again."

Parvana plopped the howling Hassan into Asif's lap. "You think you can do better? Go ahead and try."

Hassan immediately stopped crying. Parvana stared, open-mouthed, as the rage disappeared from Asif's face when Hassan's little fingers reached up and grabbed his nose.

"Go find my crutches," he said to Parvana.

She was about to yell at him for ordering her about, but the crutches seemed like a good idea.

"Where are they?"

"If I knew, I wouldn't tell you to go and look for them," he said with annoying logic.

She found them a little ways from the mouth of the cave. They were not together.

He must have dropped them while he was escaping from whatever was chasing him, she thought. She took the crutches down to the stream.

Asif was sitting in the stream in his clothes, holding onto Hassan. The baby gurgled as Asif rubbed him clean.

She put the crutches down and opened a bundle to take out clean clothes for Hassan. Under the baby's clothes was her spare shalwar kameez. She took that out, too, then got the bar of rose soap from her father's shoulder bag. She unwrapped the soap and put the wrapping back in the bag. It smelled nice.

"You might want this," she said, putting the soap and clothes on the edge of the stream. She added a clean diaper for Hassan. "Don't eat the soap," she couldn't help adding in a slightly nasty tone.

Asif took the soap from her, but ignored her comment. He was too busy playing with the baby.

Parvana went downstream a little ways and scrubbed Hassan's clothes with sand. She was spreading clean wet diapers in the sun to dry when Asif called out, "He's clean. Take him."

She waited for Asif to hand the baby over to her, then realized he didn't have the strength to do so. She waded into the stream and picked Hassan up.

"Now go away, so I can wash in private."

She took Hassan to the mouth of the cave and dressed him there. He looked rosy and cheerful from his bath. There still some stale bread left, and she gave him a small piece to chew on.

"Hey, stupid one. Get over here!"

I don't have to answer him, she thought.

"I said, get over here."

Parvana played a little clapping game with Hassan and ignored the boy in the stream.

"I can't remember your name," Asif said in a tone that wasn't quite so nasty.

Parvana picked up Hassan and went down to the stream. Asif had taken off his shirt and tossed it on the shore. He was slumped over, almost as though he couldn't hold himself up any more. His hair was full of soap.

Parvana fetched one of the drinking cups and waded into the stream. He turned his face away from her when she came up behind him.

She gasped when she saw the scars that criss-crossed his back. Some were old and were now a permanent part of his body. Some were fresh, still scabby and infected.

He really was being chased by a monster, Parvana thought.

"Don't just stand there," he growled.

"Put your head back." She dipped the cup into the stream. "Close your eyes," she ordered, "and your mouth." Then, doing for Asif what her mother used to do for her, she rinsed the soap out of his hair.

The effort of washing wore Asif out. He fell asleep in the sun soon after putting on Parvana's spare shalwar kameez.

With the laundry done and spread on the rocks to dry, Parvana put Hassan down on a blanket and took out her notebook and pen.

Dear Shauzia:

It's getting harder and harder to remember what you look like. Sometimes when I think of you, I can only picture you in your blue school uniform with the white chador, back when we were students in Kabul. You had long hair then. So did I.

Sometimes I put my hand behind me on my back and try to remember how far down my hair grew. I think I know, but I could be wrong.

It's hard to remember that I used to sleep in a bed and had to do my homework before I could watch television and play with my friends. It's hard to remember that we used to have ice cream and cakes to eat. Was that really me? Did I really leave a big piece of cake on my plate one day because I didn't feel like eating it? That must have been a dream. That couldn't have been my life.

My life is dust and rocks and rude boys and skinny babies, and long days of searching for my mother when I don't have the faintest idea where she might be.

SIX

Parvana swept out the little cave using her sandal as a broom. She liked the dirt floor to be smooth, even though it never stayed that way for long.

"We could fix it up," she said to herself. She would have said it to Hassan, but Hassan was with Asif down by the stream. Even though she was alone, she spoke out loud. She liked the way her quiet words bounced around in the little cave.

"We could put some shelves up in this corner," she said, running her fingers on some jagged bits of rock that could hold boards, if she could find any wood. "Maryam and I could sleep at the front, and Mother and Ali could sleep in the back so that Ali couldn't get out without crawling over us."

What about Nooria? Parvana frowned as she measured the little space with her eyes. Then she shrugged. Nooria could sleep outside.

Satisfied for the moment with the cave floor, Parvana put her sandal back on before joining the others at the stream.

"What were you doing?" Asif asked. He was twisting grass together, trying to make a little boat. Hassan was watching him.

"I was cleaning out the cave."

"Why? It's just a cave. It's stupid to clean it."

"You think you are so right all the time," Parvana said, folding her arms across her chest. "There's a lot you don't know. Maybe it's not just a cave. Maybe it's a treasure cave."

"What are you babbling about? Hassan makes more sense than you do. There's no such thing as a treasure cave."

"There is," Parvana insisted, her voice rising. "In fact, it's exactly the sort of cave Alexander the Great would have used to hide his treasure in." She waited for Asif to ask her who Alexander the Great was so she could show off how much she knew, but he just kept working on his boat

She tapped her foot several times and then told him.

"Alexander the Great was an army general

who lived a long time ago. He took treasures from every place he conquered."

"You mean he was a thief. He should have had his hands cut off."

"He wasn't a thief," Parvana insisted, although even as she was talking, she wondered if that were true. "People loved him. They gave him their treasures."

"You mean he'd ride through a town and people loved him so much they just gave him their things?"

"They did," she insisted.

"Then they were all stupid," Asif declared. "If I had treasure, I wouldn't give any of it away." He finished twisting the grass and put the little boat in the stream. The children watched it float away with the current.

"Why would he bury his treasure anyway?" Asif asked. "Why wouldn't he keep it with him?"

"Probably there was too much to carry," Parvana said. "He had so much treasure his horses were weighed down with it, and he had to bury some or their backs would break."

"So why didn't he come back for it?"

"Maybe he forgot which cave it was in.

DEBORAH ELLIS

64

Maybe he had so much treasure that he didn't even need to think about it once he buried it. How should I know?" Parvana's mind flashed briefly on the memory of her father's books, stuck in a hole in the ground, covered up with dirt. How would she ever find them again? She chased the question from her head. It was making her sad, and she didn't want to be sad when she was busy being annoyed at Asif.

"You think there's treasure in that dirty old cave?"

"I'm sure of it," Parvana said. Why wouldn't there be? The more she thought about it, the more she was certain that a box of gold coins and big jewels lay under the ground in the cave, just waiting for her to dig up.

"If there's any treasure there, it belongs to me," Asif insisted. "I found the cave first."

Parvana sputtered with anger. "You're wearing my clothes, eating my food, and that's how you say thank you? You really are a terrible boy."

"All right, all right. I'll share it with you."

"You certainly will."

Asif pulled himself up with his crutches. He only got halfway up, when he started to fall back. Parvana put her hands under his arms and gave him a boost.

"Let's go," he said.

"Where?"

"To the cave. To start digging." He shook his head with disgust. "What did you think I was talking about? Better find something to dig with." He hobbled off.

The treasure was by now so real in Parvana's imagination that she barely minded being ordered around. She found a couple of good-sized rocks with points at the ends, picked up Hassan and joined Asif in the cave.

The floor soon lost its smoothness as Parvana and Asif scraped away at it with their rocks. Sometimes one of their rocks hit a clunk, and they got very excited until they realized they had only hit another rock.

"What will you do with your share of the treasure?" she asked Asif.

"Horses," he answered. "I'll buy lots of horses, fast ones. I'll ride and ride, and when the horse I'm riding gets tired, I'll buy another one, then another, then another. I'll never have to stop moving."

"What about food?"

"What will I need food for? I'll be riding, not walking."

"I'll buy a big house," Parvana said. "A magic house where bombs just slip off the roof without exploding. It will be a white stone house just like the one I used to live in, only bigger, with a separate house in the yard for my sister Nooria, so I wouldn't have to see her all the time. And I'll wear beautiful clothes and lots of jewels, and I'll have lots of servants so I'll never have to do housework again." She could see herself in her mind, dressed up in a glowing red shalwar kameez like the one her aunt made her that she had to sell, long ago in Kabul, so that her family could buy food to eat.

"All the jewels in the world wouldn't make you look pretty," Asif said. "What good are jewels, anyway? You can't eat them or burn them to keep you warm at night, or — "

Parvana's rock suddenly clunked against a hard surface.

"I think I've found something."

"It's just another rock."

She scraped away some more dirt. "No, I don't think so." She dug in harder. "I think it's a box!"

Asif dug his rock in close to hers. "It is! It is a box!"

They dug faster and faster, dirt flying up and around the cave.

"Watch out for Hassan. He's right behind you," Parvana managed to say while she was huffing and puffing with exertion. Asif adjusted his digging so the dirt wouldn't fly near the baby.

Bit by bit, the box emerged. Parvana got up onto her knees to pull it out, and Asif leaned in to help. With a giant grunt, they pulled the box out of the ground. It was made of green metal, twice as long as Parvana's sandal and one sandal width wide.

"It's smaller than I thought a treasure box would be," Asif said.

"Diamonds don't have to be big," Parvana replied. "Let's take it out in the sun so that the jewels will really sparkle when we open it." She dragged the box out of the cave into the sunshine. While Asif scooted out on his bottom, she went back for Hassan, so he could be there for the treasure-box opening, too.

Asif pounded on the dirt-encrusted lock with a rock until it broke apart.

"It's rusty," he said.

"It's been under the ground for thousands of years," Parvana said. "You'd be rusty, too."

Asif pulled the broken pieces of padlock away from the clasp.

"Ready?"

"Ready." She put her hands near his, and they opened the box together.

It was full of bullets.

The children looked down and stared, too shocked to speak. Hassan gurgled and reached out to touch the shiny little objects.

Asif slammed the box shut.

"Some treasure," he yelled. "Why do I listen to you?" He pulled himself up on his crutches, yanking away from Parvana's offer of help. He knocked her with his shoulder as he hobbled away from the cave.

Parvana opened the box again. Maybe her eyes had played tricks on her.

But they hadn't. All she saw were rows of tightly packed bullets, and when she ran her hands through them, no jewels winked out at her. Only bullets.

They weren't buried by Alexander the Great. Bullets hadn't been invented back then.

They were probably buried by the men who had fought in the war that had started long before she was born. Maybe the man who buried them had died. Maybe he forgot which cave they were in. Maybe he had so many bullets he didn't need these.

It didn't matter. There was no treasure.

With great effort, Parvana lifted the box over her head and threw it as far away as she could. It landed with a thud, the bullets spilling out over the ground. They looked like seeds on the earth, but Parvana knew they would not turn into food.

She picked up Hassan and sat with him, looking away from the cave. She turned Hassan so that he couldn't see her face. She was ashamed of herself for getting caught up in a stupid dream, as though she were still a child.

SEVEN

"I'm leaving tomorrow," Parvana told Asif the next morning. They had all slept outside. Parvana didn't feel like smoothing down the floor of the cave again. She didn't feel like being reminded of her foolishness.

"Where are you going?" Asif asked.

"To look for my mother."

"But where are you going to look?"

Parvana gazed around and picked a direction. "Over that way."

"Why that way?"

"Because it's part of my plan."

"You have a plan?"

"Of course I have a plan." Parvana's only plan was to keep walking in the hopes of bumping into her mother somewhere. "But I see no reason to tell you what it is."

"I don't want to know anyway," Asif said. "It's probably a stupid plan."

It will be wonderful to leave you behind,

Parvana thought. How lovely and quiet my days and nights will be.

"I suppose you think I'm going to come with you," Asif said.

Parvana pretended she didn't hear him.

"I suppose you think I'd be grateful to go with you," Asif continued. "I suppose you think I can't look after myself out here."

Parvana kept quiet, feeling very superior for having the patience to not answer back.

She decided to wash all the clothes so everything would be clean when she started walking again.

Asif kicked at the ground with his one leg. "I suppose you'll take the baby."

"You want me to leave him with you?"

"I don't care."

Parvana picked up Hassan and the soiled diapers and carried them down to the stream. She was still scrubbing the first diaper when she heard Asif's crutches coming up behind her.

"You'll probably walk right by your mother," he said. "You'll be walking in one direction, and she'll be walking in another, and you'll pass right by each other and keep on walking forever and ever until you both run out of ground to walk on," Asif said. "It makes more sense for you to stay here. Your mother will probably walk by here any day looking for you. In fact, I think she'll come soon, and she'll be very angry when I tell her you couldn't wait around for her."

"What makes you think my mother will be here soon?" Parvana asked. Could he be right? She felt a flicker of hope.

"Just a feeling," Asif replied. "Do you want to take that chance?"

He doesn't know anything, she realized. He's just talking. She felt disappointed but not surprised.

She washed the rest of the diapers and spread them out to dry. "I wish you could wash out your own diapers," she said to Hassan.

Hassan reached for a shiny stone, ignoring Parvana's complaints.

"It would probably really annoy you if I came with you, wouldn't it?" Asif said. "You'd probably hate it. You're probably wishing and wishing that I'll stay behind."

Parvana smoothed the wrinkles out of one of the washed diapers. She didn't say anything.

"In that case," Asif said, "I'll come. Just to annoy you."

Parvana felt a strange, surprising relief. She had known, deep inside, that she wouldn't have been able to leave him behind.

"Please don't," she said.

"Forget it," he said. "My mind is made up. And don't try to sneak away without me, because I'll catch you, and you'll be sorry."

The idea of Asif catching up with anything faster than a worm almost made her smile, but she caught herself in time. She got her shoulder bag and sat down to write to her friend.

Dear Shauzia:

We're moving away from here tomorrow. I like staying in one place, but each time I do, it gets harder to leave. After all the moving around that I've done, I should be used to it. But I'm not.

We have to leave, though. We're running out of food. We're down to four scoops of rice and a bit of oil.

I don't know if there will be food where we're going, but I do know there won't be any more here.

Maybe we'll find a really wonderful place with lots of food, and grownups who can look after Hassan, and a room I can sleep in that's far away from everyone who bothers me.

Was I always this grumpy?

I hope there's lots of food where you are. I wish you could send us some.

Until next time,
Your friend,
Parvana

The next morning, Parvana washed out the diapers Hassan had dirtied again and wrapped them in a cloth. She would spread them out to dry when they stopped for a rest.

She started to bundle up the food.

"What if there's no water where we're going?" Asif asked. "How will you cook the rice? You didn't think of that, did you?"

She hadn't, although she hated to admit it. She took the cook-pot out of the bundle.

"I guess I should cook it all up now," she said. "I don't like to do that. I don't know how long it will last without growing moldy if it's cooked."

"We'll eat it before it gets moldy," Asif said. "There's not that much left."

Parvana knew he was right. Four little cups of rice would not last long with two children and one baby eating it. She gathered some grasses and dried weeds. Asif broke them into the right size, struck a match, and soon had a fire going. Parvana fetched water, and they cooked the rice.

"We could eat some while it's hot, couldn't we?" Asif asked.

Parvana thought that would be a good idea. "We'll only eat a little bit," she said. "It's got to last until we find more food."

They ate the hot rice right out of the pot. Hassan sat on Asif's lap, and Asif fed him, too.

It seemed like they had just started eating when Parvana noticed the pot was only half filled with rice.

"Stop eating!" she cried, snatching the pot away from Asif's hands. "This has got to last!"

"Why did you eat so much, then?"

"Don't blame me! You're the one who kept shoveling it in, as if we were rich people with bags of rice all over the place." Parvana flung her arm so violently in anger that the pot of rice slipped out of her fingers and flew off into the dirt.

It landed bottom up.

Neither child spoke. They stared at the up-turned pot.

After a long, terrible moment, Parvana walked over to the pot and carefully lifted it up. Most of the rice was still stuck to the bottom. She must have cooked it too long.

There was still some rice on the ground. Asif shuffled over on his behind, and together they picked up the rice, grain by grain, and put it back in the pot.

When everything was packed up, Parvana took out her notebook.

Dear Shauzia:
I hate it when I make things worse. Why do I behave so badly? Why can't I be nice?

She helped Asif stand up, picked up the bundles and the baby, and the children walked away from the cave. They didn't look back.

EIGHT

They walked for two days before the food ran out, and then they walked for two days more.

Parvana's belly had that ache it got when she didn't feed it. It was a mixture of pain and emptiness. Her head felt empty, too, and she felt dull and stupid.

Hassan wailed the first day after the rice was gone, but by the second day the wail had dwindled to a thin whine, like the sound he had been making when Parvana first found him.

"Hassan needs to rest," Asif said. Parvana suspected it was Asif who needed to rest, but he would never admit that. He moved more and more slowly, and his face had the same expression her father's face had when he was in pain.

Parvana put Hassan on the ground, then her bundles. She held onto Asif's arm as he sat down. When he was tired, he often slipped and rolled onto his side when he was trying to sit. This embarrassed him and made him grumpy.

"Is there any water left?" Asif asked.

Parvana untied the bundle with the plastic water bottle in it and shook the bottle so Asif could hear that there was still a bit sloshing around. He reached out his hand, and she passed it over.

She was going to remind him to take it easy, to not drink too much, but what was the point? It didn't make any difference whether Asif took two swallows or one. They still needed to find more water soon.

Asif poured a little bit of water into the cap of the bottle. Parvana watched him pour it, bit by bit, into Hassan's mouth, not spilling any.

"Isn't that good?" he asked. "Would you like some more?" He gave Hassan three capfuls of water before taking a swallow himself. Then he passed the water bottle back to Parvana.

"Do you have any brothers or sisters?" Parvana asked Asif. She realized that she didn't know anything about this boy who was traveling with her. She knew he came out of a cave, but she didn't know where he came from before that. She knew he was annoying, but she didn't know why. She didn't know who had hated him enough to tear up his back.

"I'm alone," Asif replied shortly.

"So am I," Parvana said, "but I've got family somewhere. What about you? Do you have a family somewhere else?"

Asif tried to get Hassan to play with his finger, but Hassan didn't seem interested in playing. He didn't seem interested in anything.

"No," Asif said finally.

"Did they go away? What happened to them?"

"I had a family. Now I don't. That's all there is." He wouldn't say any more, and Parvana wondered why she'd bothered to ask.

She took out her notebook.

Dear Shauzia:

Another day of being hungry, with nothing around that looks like food. I don't even know if I am hungry any more. I'm just tired, and I feel like crying all the time. We're almost out of water, and I don't know what to do.

Remember those fairy stories we read in school, where someone taps a magic wand on a rock and water pours out of it, or where someone rubs a lamp and a genie comes out to grant three wishes? I believed in that when I was little, but now I know that a rock is just a rock, and that rubbing a lamp only makes it shiny.

Maybe when I'm old and spend all my time dreaming in the sun, I'll be able to believe in those things again. But what do I believe in until then?

"You're not very smart," Asif said, "to be carrying all those things in your bag. It's tiring you out and making you mean. You're stupid."

Parvana slammed down her notebook. "How dare you call me stupid? I *have* to carry all these things. Who else is going to carry them?"

"I could carry something. I could carry Hassan."

"Don't be silly. You can barely walk."

"I could carry him on my back. It's not so sore now." Asif took off his blanket shawl and tied it into a sort of a sling. "Hassan can sit in here, and I'll tie this end around my neck."

Parvana thought of her aching arms. "Do you think it will work?"

"Of course it will work. I've been thinking about it for awhile."

They tried it out. Parvana had to help Asif stand, and she had to tie the baby sling on him, but it did appear to work all right. Hassan didn't seem to care. He whimpered, but he whimpered when Parvana carried him, too, so she didn't think it was because he was on Asif's back instead of in her arms.

Asif could still manage his crutches with the baby on his back, so the three children moved on. They followed a dirt road because it was flat and easier to walk on. Sometimes a truck went by, or a donkey cart, but although Parvana waved for them to stop, they just kept going.

Toward the end of the day they came to a tiny village, almost as small as the one Hassan had come from. This one hadn't been bombed or, if it had, the people had long since rebuilt it.

Old men sat on the ground outside their homes, shading their eyes from the sun as they watched Parvana, Asif and Hassan move slowly down the middle of the road that ran through the village. Parvana felt uncomfortable with their eyes on her, but there was nothing she could do about it.

"Do you think we should ask them for water?" she whispered to Asif.

"They don't look very friendly. They might ask a lot of questions and make trouble for us," Asif said. "Let's see if we can find someone else to ask. Maybe we can find a child."

They saw a few small boys playing with an oddly shaped soccer ball. There wasn't enough air in it, and it didn't go very far when they kicked it.

"Where can we get some water?" Asif asked them.

"There's a tea house down there," one of the soccer players said. "Do you want to play with us?"

"I'm thirsty," Asif said. "Maybe later."

The boys went back to their game. Parvana and Asif walked a little farther down the road and came to the tea shop.

"We don't have any money," Parvana said. "We'll have to beg."

"I don't beg," Asif said. "I can work."

Parvana sighed. She was too tired to work. Begging would have been much easier.

The tea shop was a little mud hut with a few tables in it. There were three men inside sitting in silence. A large tea urn was at one end of the room.

Shauzia had been a tea-boy back in Kabul, running around the marketplace delivering trays full of cups of tea to merchants in their stalls. But there didn't seem a need for that sort of person in this village.

"We're looking for work," Asif said.

One of the men shifted in his chair. "There's no work here, boy. Do you think we'd be sitting still if there was work available?"

"We'll do anything," Parvana said, "and you don't have to pay us. Just give us something to eat and drink."

The man took a swallow of tea and took his time answering, as though Parvana and Asif were well-fed children asking for work for the fun of it.

"You can't work," he finally said, looking at Asif.

"My brother will look after the baby," Parvana said quickly. "I can do the work of two."

"What is your name?" the man asked.

"Kaseem," Parvana replied, giving her boy-name.

"My chicken house needs cleaning," he said. "If you do a good job of that, I'll give you some food, but then you'll have to be on your way. I only have one chicken house, and I'm not about to give away food for free."

The chicken house stood at the back of the small yard. It was filthy.

"There's water there if you want a drink," the man said, pointing at a rain barrel. "If the water's good enough for the chickens, it's good enough for you. I'll bring you food when you finish the work." And he went back to his friends.

The yard was surrounded by a fence that was falling apart more than it was standing up, although the fence around the chicken house was in good repair. Parvana lifted Hassan off Asif's back and helped the two of them settle in a bit of shade under two scraggly trees. She brought them a ladle of water, but Asif motioned for her to drink first. She emptied the ladle in a second, then filled it again. Asif gave some to Hassan before drinking himself.

Parvana thought of the chickens that had bullied her in the bombed-out village. She wasn't in the mood to be bullied today, and the chickens seemed to sense that. They scurried out of her way.

She worked steadily, scraping away chicken muck with an old board and pushing filthy straw out into the yard, trying not to get too much muck on herself. As soon as she got the job done, they could eat.

Nestled in some straw, she found some eggs the owner had forgotten to collect. How could she take them? They would show, and probably break, if she put them in her pocket. She looked over at Asif, asleep with Hassan, using their blanket bundle as a pillow.

Parvana looked around. It was wrong to steal. She had seen what happened to thieves under Taliban law. They had their hands cut off. She didn't want that to happen to her. But she did want those eggs!

She cupped the eggs in her hands and checked to make sure the coast was clear. She would dash across the yard, tuck the eggs into the blanket bundle and dash back into the hen house.

But she couldn't do it. Her father would not be proud of her if she stole. They were often hungry when they were traveling together, and although the opportunity to steal came up, her father wouldn't hear of it. "Our bellies would be full tonight," he would say, "but could we live with ourselves in the morning?"

Parvana put the eggs back and went back to cleaning the hen house. It was filthy, but at least it was small, and soon she was finished.

"Here is your food," the man said, bringing a small bowl of rice into the yard.

"There are three of us," Parvana said.

"But only one of you worked. Do I look like a rich man?"

"You are richer than we are," Parvana said. "We are children."

"If I help all the hungry children in Afghanistan, I would soon be as poor as you. If you don't want the rice, I'll take it away."

"We want it," Asif said. But the man stood there and held the bowl just out of Asif's reach.

"Please," Asif said. "Can we please have the rice." Parvana could see his hand trembling.

The man finally handed the bowl to Asif, then went back inside.

The children shared the small amount of rice, eating in grim silence. It didn't take long to empty the bowl. Then Parvana filled their water bottles, and Asif rinsed out a few diapers for Hassan.

"Grownups shouldn't turn their backs on children," he said angrily as he squeezed water out of the diapers.

"I wish I had taken those eggs of his," Parvana muttered, casting a dark look at the tea house.

"Go and get them now," Asif said.

"It's too risky."

"Then we'll come back."

They found a spot at the edge of town where they couldn't be seen. They spread the diapers out to dry and waited until night came.

Leaving Hassan asleep in the hiding spot with their belongings, Parvana and Asif snuck back into the village and into the back yard of the tea house.

Parvana found the eggs she had left behind and put them into her shoulder bag next to her letters to Shauzia.

Asif, moving slowly, picked up a chicken so smoothly and calmly that the chicken didn't even squawk. He put his shawl around it and handed it to Parvana. Then they crept out of the yard.

On the edge of the village, they picked up Hassan and their belongings and kept walking until the village was far behind them.

"People who cheat children deserve to have bad things happen to them," Parvana said. "I don't feel the least bit sorry."

"Eggs for breakfast," said Asif.

Then they laughed.

NINE

Parvana couldn't sleep. Her belly was empty, and it hurt.

When they had the chicken and the eggs, it felt like they had all the food in the world. Hassan couldn't eat chicken very well because he only had a few teeth to chew with, so Parvana and Asif decided to let him have the eggs. Parvana cooked them up nice and soft. There was no oil left to cook with, but she watched them carefully, and they did not stick to the pan too badly.

Asif killed the chicken simply and quickly, and Parvana began to think there were things he could do besides complain and annoy her.

They ate the chicken for as long as they could, feeding Hassan the softer parts. They all felt better when they were eating. Hassan took an interest in things again, and Parvana wasn't nearly so grumpy.

But eventually there was nothing left to eat, and they all became hungry again.

Had it been a week since the chicken ran out? Parvana could no longer keep track of time. She lay on the hard ground, wondering what the point was of eating one day, when they just got hungry again the next day.

She closed her eyes and tried again to sleep.

She had chosen her sleeping spot carelessly. There was a rock in the ground that jutted into her back. No matter how she changed her position, she was still uncomfortable. But the night was cold, and at least she was warm. If she got up to find a more comfortable place, she'd get cold. If she stayed warm, she'd be uncomfortable.

At least she didn't have to worry about waking Hassan if she got up. He slept with Asif all the time now.

The rock dug into her again, and she decided to move. She could always get warm again.

"One, two, three," she whispered, then flung back her blanket.

The cold air grabbed at her. She tried to move quickly before it really chilled her, but she couldn't find a smooth place to put her blanket. So she wrapped her blanket around her shoulders and sat on the ground.

"Maybe I'm the only person awake in the whole world," she whispered. "Everyone else is sleeping and dreaming, and I'm awake, watching over all of them. Parvana the Protector." She smiled.

She started humming a song about the moon that she had learned at school. The music went out into the cold night air and seemed to make the stars twinkle more brightly.

There was a shuffling behind her. She knew without turning that Asif was awake, and she waited for him to say something rude about her singing.

Instead, he shuffled over to her on his bottom. He gently tugged at the corner of her blanket, and she wrapped it around both their shoulders. She added words to the song she'd been humming. Then Asif sang something he knew, then they sang something together that they both knew.

They sat and sang and watched for shooting stars, until they were both so tired they were able to fall asleep again, even with the ache in their empty bellies and the sharp rocks under their backs.

TEN

*D*ear *Shauzia:*
   We're going to have to walk again today,
although I would rather just sit. I'm so tired.
But I keep thinking of what my father always
said. "If we stop, we die."
   Hassan flops around. He's like a sack of
rice. His eyes are dull, and he doesn't respond
when we talk to him. It's like he's already gone
away.
   The grass we ate yesterday upset our stom-
achs. We all have nasty stuff pouring out the
bottom of us. It's bad enough for Asif and me,
but it's worse for Hassan, who has no clean
clothes left. It's a good thing the sun is warm
today, because he's naked until his laundry
dries. One of us has to keep fanning him to
keep the flies away.

Wait a minute, Parvana thought. Hassan
hadn't eaten any grass. They had tried to feed

him some, but he wouldn't take it. So why was he sick?

Then she knew. She had forgotten to boil the water before they drank it.

She knew well enough to do that. Even back in Kabul, where the water came from a tap in the street, it had to be boiled before you could drink it. Unboiled water could make people sick. Everybody knew that.

She looked out at the little pond they'd been living beside and drinking from for three days. Fast-moving streams were sometimes safe, but water in ponds always had to be boiled. How many times had her father told her that? No wonder they were all sick.

She took up her pen again.

I'm tired of having to remember things. I want someone else to do the remembering.

Parvana put her writing things back in her shoulder bag and gathered some dried grasses to build a fire so she could boil some water. Until someone else came along, she would have to take care of things.

"At least with our stomachs upset, we don't

feel like eating," she said, when the baby's clothes had dried and they were walking again.

Asif didn't answer. It seemed to take all of his energy to simply keep moving. Parvana knew she should carry Hassan for him, but she didn't offer.

Two more days passed. The children stopped for yet another rest.

Parvana sat with her writing things in her lap. She was going to write another letter to Shauzia, but couldn't bear to write again about how hungry they were, or how thirsty, or how much Hassan stank. She was tired of writing those things. She wanted to be able to write something new.

If only the world were different, she thought. She closed her eyes and imagined a cool, green valley, like the one her mother's family came from, only better and brighter than the way her mother had described it. She thought of the sort of place where she would like to live. Then she opened her eyes and began to write.

Dear Shauzia:
This morning we came to a hidden valley in

the Afghan mountains, so secret that only chil-
dren can find it. It's all green, except where it's
blue or yellow or red, or other colors I don't
even know the names of. The colors are so
bright you think at first they will hurt your
eyes, but they don't. It's all so restful.

Parvana kept writing, and as her words
filled the page, she could see Green Valley
more clearly in her mind. It almost became
real.

"Writing to your friend again?" Asif asked
from where he was sitting.

"Do you want to hear it?"

"Why would I want to hear what a couple
of girls have to say to each other?"

"You'll like this," Parvana said. "Let me
read it to you."

Asif didn't say yes, but he didn't say no, so
Parvana read out what she had written.

Green Valley is full of food. Every day we
eat like we are celebrating the end of Ramadan.
I just finished eating a big platter of Kabuli rice
with lots of raisins and big hunks of roasted
lamb buried inside it. After that I ate an orange

as big as my head and three bowls of strawberry ice cream. No one in Afghanistan has ice cream any more, except for the children of Green Valley, and we can have as much as we want.

You would love it here. Maybe when you get tired of France you could come here, and this is where we could meet instead of the Eiffel Tower. Now that I've found this place, I never want to leave.

We can drink the water here without boiling it, and we don't get sick. The other children tell me it's magic water. All the children here have both arms and legs. No one is blind, and no one is unhappy. Maybe Asif's leg will even grow back.

Parvana finished reading. She sighed deeply and put the letter down. It sounded foolish. While she was writing it, she could see everything so clearly! But now she could only think about her empty belly, Asif's terrible cough and blown-off leg, and the horrible smell coming from Hassan.

"Green Valley." Asif kicked at the dirt with his foot. "There's no such place."

"No," Parvana said flatly. "There's no such place. I made it up."

"Why?"

Parvana shrugged. "I just thought... I guess I just thought that if I could imagine it, I could make it real."

"Just like Alexander the Great's treasure in the cave," Asif taunted.

Parvana was furious with herself for sharing her dream with Asif, but mostly for having a dream in the first place. His leg would not grow back, there would never be enough food, and unboiled water would always make people sick.

She ripped the paper out of the notebook, balled it up and threw it into the field.

A breeze picked up the little ball of paper and sent it back to her. It landed just out of her reach.

She picked up a stone and threw it at the paper. She missed, then threw another stone angrily.

"Those are lousy throws," Asif said.

"Oh, you think you could do better with those skinny arms of yours?"

"I could throw better than you if I had no arms!"

The challenge was on. Parvana helped Asif stand up, and she handed him some stones. He leaned on one crutch as he threw. His first throw went a lot farther than hers.

"I told you!"

"My first throws didn't count," Parvana insisted. "I wasn't trying." She threw another rock. This was much better.

They kept throwing. Sometimes Asif's throw went farther, sometimes hers did. She kept handing Asif rocks, and he kept throwing them.

"Anyone can throw these small stones," Asif said. "Get me some big rocks, and I'll show you how to really throw."

Parvana made a little pile of rocks big enough to need two hands to throw. She had to hold him up while he threw these, because he couldn't throw and hold onto his crutches at the same time. The effort made him cough, but he kept trying.

Parvana picked up the largest rock in the pile. It was quite heavy. She put all her strength behind it and heaved it into the field.

The ground roared and rose up in front of them, as if a monster was punching its way through from below.

The children screamed. They screamed and screamed, and kept screaming as the dust settled.

Asif threw a stone at Parvana's shoulder. "You led us into a mine field!" he hollered, his rage making his voice even louder than Hassan's screams. "You are the stupidest girl. With all your writing and all your France, you don't know what you're doing! We will all be blown up! You are stupid, stupid, stupid!" As he yelled at her, his hand kept grabbing at the place where his leg used to be.

Something made Parvana put her arms around Asif's frail body. They dropped to the ground, gathered up the stinking, weeping Hassan, clung to each other, and cried and cried.

ELEVEN

Parvana didn't know how long they sat like that. It seemed like hours and it seemed like minutes.

She shielded her eyes and looked out at the rocky, dusty field. She couldn't tell by looking at it how deadly it was.

Sometimes land mines were spread on top of the ground, brightly painted to look like pretty things. People would try to pick them up and get their arms blown off. Most of the land mines were buried just a few inches under the ground. People didn't know they were stepping on them until the bombs exploded.

Parvana didn't know what to do now. If they were in a mine field, all they had to do was take one wrong step, and the earth would rise up beneath them.

Should they head out across the field and maybe get blown up? Should they stay where they were and wait to die from hunger and thirst? How could she know what was the right decision? She was too tired and sad to even guess. Either way, it looked as though they were all going to die. She would never meet up with Shauzia after all. She thought of her friend, sitting at the top of the Eiffel Tower, waiting and waiting and waiting.

Parvana rested her chin on Asif's shoulder as their crying subsided into quiet sobbing. She looked out at the field. All she saw was rocks and dust and hills with more rocks and dust.

Something caught her eye. It was moving toward them. She blinked a few times to be sure she was seeing correctly, then sat up straight.

"Someone's coming," she said, "across the mine field."

Asif turned and looked where she was pointing.

"I think it's a girl," he said.

"I think you're right," Parvana said, seeing the chador flow out from the girl's head as she ran toward them.

"Do you think she's real?" Asif asked.

Parvana wasn't prepared to guess. Things

that seemed real to her turned out to be things she had just dreamed up.

"We can't both be imagining her, can we?"

Before they had time to wonder, the girl herself was there.

"Children!" she exclaimed. "It's been ages since I've seen children!" She bent down to hug them.

Parvana and Asif were too stunned to hug her back.

The girl was smaller than Asif. She wore a filthy green chador over her hair. "And you have a baby. Oh, this is wonderful! Did anybody die?"

Parvana's brain, sluggish from hunger, was slow to respond.

"What?"

"The explosion," the girl said, waving her hands in the air. "Is anybody dead?"

"No, no, there's no one dead."

"What's the baby's name?" the girl asked.

Asif answered. "His name is Hassan."

"It's too bad you're all boys," she said. "I've been wanting and wanting a sister."

"She's a girl," Asif said, jerking his thumb at Parvana.

"Are you? You're a very strange-looking girl."

Asif giggled. Parvana frowned at him. She could say the same about this girl. She wore a dress that looked like a long piece of flowered cloth with a hole cut out for her head. Her belt was a rope. Her face was covered with sores like the ones Parvana had seen on other children. Her father had told her they came from disease and infection. The girl wore an assortment of bangles and necklaces made from objects Parvana couldn't completely identify — a nail in the necklace, and something that looked like the twisty end of a broken lightbulb. The jewelry clanked and jingled as the girl pranced around them.

Parvana felt too overwhelmed by the girl's energy to ask her any questions.

"Well, let's go," the girl said.

"Go where?"

"To my house, of course. I always take what I find in the mine field back to my house. You are even better than a wagon or a donkey. Have you ever eaten donkey? Of course, I couldn't get the whole donkey home. I had to cut off a bit of it, just big enough to carry. I came back for more, but by then the flies and the buzzards had found it. I don't like to eat things if the flies have been on it, and those buzzards scare me."

The girl kept talking as she picked up the two bundles and walked away, leaving Parvana to pick up Hassan and Asif to pick up himself.

"Wait!" Parvana called after her. "What about the land mines?"

"Land mines won't hurt me," the girl called back. "Just follow me and they won't hurt you, either."

The girl headed out across the mine field. She moved so quickly, skipping along, that Parvana had to call her a few times to wait for them. The mine field was dotted with animal skeletons, broken wagon wheels and bits of soft-drink bottles.

The girl led them down a short canyon and into a small clearing sheltered on all sides by rocky hills.

"Welcome to my house," she said, spreading her arms as if she were welcoming them to a palace.

It was the stench that hit Parvana first. The smell of rotting meat seemed trapped in the clearing. She saw half-butchered sheep and goats on the ground, covered with flies.

The house was a mud shack like many others Parvana had seen in her travels. It was coming apart in many places. The mud was patched in spots, but only a short ways up. Parvana realized that the girl, who looked to be no more than eight years old, could not reach any higher. A cloth that was more holes than material hung over the doorway.

Apart from the animal carcasses, there was litter all over the yard — broken boards, empty bottles, bits of leather harness, frayed ropes, filthy bits of cardboard and tangles of weeds. There was another smell, too. Parvana guessed the girl had been using the yard as a latrine.

There was no one else in the yard, and no one came out of the house to greet them.

"Do you live here all alone?" Parvana asked.

"Oh, no. I live here with my grandmother. Come and meet her. She'll like you a lot."

She led them into the house. It was dark inside, and it also stank.

"I've found some children, Grandmother. Isn't that wonderful? Say hello to my grandmother," she urged Parvana and Asif.

At first Parvana thought the girl had gone completely mad, that there was no one else in the room. Slowly, her eyes adjusted to the darkness of the little house.

She saw a tall cupboard, some shabby mats against the walls and a pile of clothes in the corner.

The little girl went over to the pile of clothes, knelt down and appeared to be listening to it. "Grandmother says she's very glad to see you, and to please stay as long as you like."

"We'd better take the kid with us," Asif whispered to Parvana. "She's as crazy as you are."

Parvana was about to agree with Asif when she took a closer look at the mound of clothes.

She knelt down and put her hand on it. She felt the boniness of a human spine and the slight rise and fall of breath.

The girl's grandmother was curled into a ball on a thin mattress, with her back to the door. She had a dark cloth draped over her whole body. Even her face was covered. She did not move or make a sound. Only the tiny movement of her breathing and the absence of the death smell proved to Parvana that the woman was alive.

The little girl didn't seem to notice anything was wrong. She took them back outside.

"Grandmother needs a lot of rest," she said, before twirling around in a dance of activity.

Parvana remembered that her own mother had been like that, lying on the toshak at home when her father was in jail. She remembered the woman on the hill.

This was what happened to grownups when they became too sad to keep going. She wondered whether it would ever happen to her, too.

She had a hundred questions for the girl, but for the moment she just asked one.

"What is your name?"

"Leila," the girl said, and she fetched them some water and cold rice.

The food and drink revived Parvana and Asif, but neither of them could coax Hassan to eat. He just didn't seem interested.

"He's almost dead," Leila said very matter-of-factly.

"No, he's not," Asif insisted. "He's going to be fine." He soaked the edge of his shirt with water and put it in Hassan's mouth. For a long minute it seemed as if Hassan would just let it sit there. Then he started sucking the water out.

"See? He's going to be fine." He made a paste out of a bit of rice, and Hassan ate that, too.

There was a well in the clearing with a hand pump, and they were able to wash. Leila brought out clean clothes for them.

"These were my mother's," she said.

Parvana felt very proud of herself for not laughing at Asif as he came out of the house dressed in a lady's shalwar kameez until his own clothes were washed and dried. His stick-thin body was lost in the grownup clothes, and a glower covered his whole face.

Parvana liked being back in girl clothes. The shalwar kameez Leila gave her was light blue with white embroidery down the front. It made her feel almost pretty again.

In the yard there was a cook-fire with rocks around it that made a place to set pots on. Leila cooked some rice and meat stew for supper. Before serving it, she took a pinch of food from the pot and put it in a little hole she made in the ground with her fingers. Parvana was too tired to ask what she was doing.

"It's pigeon stew," the little girl said. "I hope you like it."

Parvana wouldn't have cared if she were

eating vulture. Any food was good food. Asif spooned broth from the stew into Hassan's mouth. Hassan swallowed everything, keeping his eyes on Asif's face.

They ate their evening meal in the one-room house with Leila's grandmother. Leila talked non-stop as she put some food on a plate, lifted her grandmother's head cover a little and placed the plate underneath it.

Parvana watched closely. Eventually she saw slow movements under the cover as the old woman lifted morsels of food from her plate to her mouth.

Through it all, Leila talked and talked. Words spilled out of her like she was a pot boiling over.

"I know I'm talking a lot," she said, "but it's been such a long time since I had anyone to talk to, especially children. Of course, I have Grandmother, but she doesn't talk much."

As far as Parvana could see, Grandmother didn't talk at all.

"Was she always so quiet?" she asked Leila.

"Oh, no. She used to talk all the time. All the women in my family are big talkers. She didn't go quiet until my mother wandered off."

"Mothers don't just wander off," Asif said.

"Well, really she went looking for my brother and father. Someone came by and told us they were killed in the fighting, but she didn't believe them and went off to look for herself. She hasn't come back yet. I sit up on the hill every day and watch for her, but she hasn't come back yet." She looked confused, Parvana thought, as if she couldn't understand why her mother was taking so long.

Asif asked the question Parvana was almost too afraid to ask.

"How long ago did she leave?"

Leila seemed puzzled.

"Did she leave before last winter?" Parvana asked.

"Yes," Leila said. "Before the winter. The nights were still warm when she left."

That was months and months ago.

"You've been alone all that time?"

"Not alone," Leila insisted. "With Grandmother."

Asif and Parvana exchanged looks. Being alone with a grandmother like that was as bad as being all alone.

"Go ahead and talk all you want," Parvana said. "We'll listen."

TWELVE

They spent the night in the little house. Leila shared her mattress with Parvana, and Asif slept next to Hassan. Parvana slept deeply and did not dream.

The flies woke her up.

We'll have to do something about that, she thought as she scratched at the flea bites on her ankles. They would have to do something about the bugs in the beds, too.

She realized she had decided to stay for awhile.

The others were still sleeping. Parvana gently lifted Leila's arm from where it had fallen across her chest and went outside.

The clearing was a little world by itself. The way the hills surrounded it, it was hard to tell there was a world outside at all.

Parvana walked around the little house. In the back was a patch of dirt that looked as if it might have been a vegetable garden at one point. There were sticks in the ground that could have staked tomatoes, like the ones she had seen in gardens in the villages she had passed through with her father.

Near the garden was a rusty wire cage full of pigeons. The cage was taller than Parvana, but the perch had broken and was lying on the ground covered with droppings. Most of the pigeons hopped around in the muck on the bottom. One was trying to work its way through a hole in the wires. Parvana put her hand against the hole and felt the bird's soft head butt against her palm.

"We ate one of those last night," Leila said, coming up behind her. "We eat some, and they keep having babies, so we have more to eat."

Leila took Parvana on a tour of the clearing. "These are apple trees," she said, pointing to two scraggly trees with shiny green leaves and little green apples on the branches. "The apples will be ready in the fall. They're good, but you have to eat around the worms."

In another part of the yard were sacks of flour and rice. Parvana could see mouse holes in some of the bags.

"Come and see my treasure house," Leila said.

The treasure house turned out to be some boards leaning up against a rock. Leila pulled one of the boards away. Parvana peered in and saw cans of cooking oil, several bolts of cloth, a box of light bulbs, cooking pots, sandals of many sizes, men's caps, lengths of rope, several thermos flasks, and a box of bars of soap, some chewed by mice.

"Where did all this come from?" Parvana asked.

"A peddler got blown up in the mine field. That was a really good day. We got all these things. I made myself this dress from some of the cloth."

Parvana struggled to understand. "You mean you go out into the mine field when you hear an explosion?"

"Of course. That's how I found you."

"What happened to the peddler?"

"Oh, he was blown up. His cart and clothes were all blown up, too. Nothing there we could use. I had to make a lot of trips to carry all these things back."

Parvana had an image of Leila as a spider, waiting for a fly to become trapped in her web.

Asif had joined them in time to hear the last

part. "You actually go into the mine field? That's stupid."

Parvana frowned at him.

"He means it's dangerous."

"Not for me," Leila said. "The ground likes me. Every time I eat, I put a few crumbs in the ground to feed it. That's what keeps me safe. Oh, no, it's not dangerous for me. Do what I do, and it won't be dangerous for you, either."

"You're a little bit crazy, aren't you?" Asif said.

"Pay no attention to him," Parvana said, putting her arm around the girl's shoulder. "He's always in a bad mood."

"You two belong together," Asif said over his shoulder as he hobbled away to answer Hassan's call from inside the house. "You're both dreamers."

Leila smiled at Parvana.

"Let's be sisters," she said.

Being sisters sounded fine to Parvana.

"All right. We'll be sisters."

"Can your brothers be my brothers?"

"You mean Asif and Hassan? They're not my brothers. We just sort of found each other."

"That makes them your brothers," Leila said.

"Yes, I guess it does," Parvana agreed, and

she wondered how Asif would feel about having her for a sister.

"And that makes them *my* brothers, and my grandmother is *your* grandmother."

Parvana didn't say how she felt about having a lump on a mattress for a grandmother. It didn't matter. A grandmother was a grandmother, and it was nice to have one.

"Who taught you to cook and take care of things?" Parvana asked.

"I used to watch my brother and father do things before they went off to the war. My grandmother and my mother taught me other things, and some things I just made up." Leila skipped off to build the fire up to make the morning tea.

Parvana found Asif shuffling through a pile of broken bits of board by the pigeon house.

"I think I'd like to stay here for awhile," she told him.

"If you think I'm going to stay here with that crazy girl and her crazy grandmother, you're as crazy as they are."

"I didn't ask you to stay," Parvana said. "I just said I'm staying. Hassan, too," she added.

"You're probably hoping I'll go," Asif said. "It will probably make you miserable if I stay."

Parvana knew what was coming. She kept quiet.

"So I will stay," Asif decided, "but only because it will annoy you." He poked a crutch at the rubble one more time before walking away.

Parvana sighed. He really was a tiresome boy.

Dear Shauzia:

We've found a real Green Valley. It's a little rough still, and it will take a lot of work to make it beautiful, but we can do it.

This is a place where children are safe. No one is hurt or beaten or taken away in the night. Everyone is kind to everyone else, and no one is afraid.

We won't let the war in here. We'll build a place that is happy and free, and if any war people come they will feel too good to keep on killing.

Parvana looked around the clearing. There was so much work to do. She smiled.

They would begin by cleaning up the yard.

THIRTEEN

Parvana kept her plan to herself for the first few days. She and Asif needed to rest and take care of Hassan, and she wanted Leila to get used to them before she started changing things.

She did use an old board to scoop dirt over the animal carcasses. They'd have to be properly buried, but she didn't have the strength to do that just yet.

"The dirt might help keep the flies away," she explained to Leila, who had taken to following her everywhere.

"I never thought of that," Leila said. "Nobody told me." She looked down at her feet. "I try to do things right."

Parvana bent down so she could look Leila in the eye. "You do all kinds of things right," she said. "If you don't know, you don't know. No shame in that."

Parvana brushed some hair out of the little

girl's face so Leila could see her smile. She suddenly drew back and then forced herself to look again.

Underneath the hair that fell over Leila's forehead was a large sore, like the smaller ones on the lower part of her face. But this one had small white worms wiggling in it.

"Come with me," she said, and she led Leila to a sunny place in the yard.

"What are you up to?" Asif asked.

Parvana showed him the sore.

"Let me take care of it," he said. "I've got more patience than you do."

Parvana was about to argue, but she realized that he was right. He was more patient. She went to heat up some water to wash the wound. That was what her mother always did.

"Do you realize you've got worms crawling in your face?" she heard Asif ask Leila.

"Sometimes I feel them and I try to brush them away, but I can't always feel them."

Parvana fetched a bit of soap from the treasure house and built up the fire under a pot of water. She cut some strips of cloth and carried everything over to Leila and Asif. On her way, she checked on Hassan. He was napping in the little house, not far from Grandmother.

"You'll need these," Parvana said to Asif and Leila. But they didn't even hear her. Leila was talking a mile a minute while Asif patiently pulled the tiny worms from her wound.

"It's the flies," he said. "They lay eggs in the sore, and the eggs grow into worms."

"How did you get to be so smart?" Leila asked.

Anyone knows that, Parvana was about to say, then bit her words back. Asif was actually smiling.

"I can take over," Parvana said.

"Why? We don't need you." Asif finished with the worms and gently dabbed at the wound with a cloth soaked in hot water. "You need to keep your face clean," he said to Leila. "In fact, you need to keep your whole self clean."

"I know I should," she said. "Now that you're all here, I will. When it was just Grandmother and me, I forgot."

Parvana left them to it. She wasn't sure what she was feeling. Was she jealous? Of what? Mentally, she gave herself a kick. Here they were, finally safe, with food to eat and water to drink, and she was getting all moody. What was wrong with her?

Whatever it was, she couldn't understand it yet. What she could understand was work. She changed into her old boy-clothes so she wouldn't get the girl-clothes dirty, and got busy.

Bit by bit, Green Valley took shape. The worst job was hauling the animal carcasses out of the clearing and burying them outside the canyon. Asif attached ropes to them, Parvana and Leila pulled them out, and all three children dug the holes. Then they dug a proper latrine and cleaned up the yard of everything that attracted flies. There was a lot less buzzing after that.

"How do you know how to do all this?" Leila asked after every new thing they did.

Parvana wasn't sure. "My mother liked everything to be clean, and she always made me help her. I also saw how people did things in the camps and villages I traveled through with my father. And some things are just common sense."

"You? Common sense?" Asif laughed.

Parvana ignored him. She had come to the

conclusion that Asif could be pleasant to everyone but her.

"We need to keep the mice out of the rice and flour," he said. He rummaged through the junk in the yard until he came up with enough boards and plastic sheeting to build some mouse-proof containers. He used rope to bind them together when he couldn't find enough nails.

"You girls clean out the rest of the rice and flour," he ordered, "and I'll make plastic pouches for the food that's still good."

Parvana noticed that Asif was always cheerful when he was giving orders.

Parvana and Leila hauled the mouse-tunneled sacks up to the top of the look-out hill.

"We can watch for my mother while we clean the rice," Leila said. "We can watch for your mother at the same time."

"Why not?" Parvana replied, flicking a mouse turd down the hill.

"Maybe your mother and my mother will meet each other, and they'll come walking across the field together. Wouldn't that be great?"

"It would be great, but it's not likely to happen."

"But it *could* happen," Leila insisted. "Don't you think so? Don't you think it *could* happen?"

"All right," Parvana relented. "It could happen."

This set Leila off on a long, detailed fantasy about how their mothers would meet and mysteriously know their children were together and decide it was time to come back to them. By the time she stopped to catch a breath, Parvana almost believed her.

"Asif's mother is dead," Leila said. "So is his father. So is everyone else."

"How do you know that?"

"He told me. He was living with an uncle who beat him, so he ran away."

"Why did he tell you? He never told me," Parvana said, but Leila was already talking about something else. Parvana stopped listening. She was too busy being annoyed at Asif.

As the days went by, Green Valley began to look better, and so did the children. Leila's sores started to heal, and one day Parvana washed and combed out the little girl's long hair. She didn't have a real comb and had to use her fingers, but Leila's hair looked much better when she was finished. Parvana tied it in two long braids and laughed as Leila swung her head from side to side, feeling the braids move.

Hassan lost the floppy-baby look.

"He's like a plant," Parvana said. "If you don't water a plant, it wilts, but then when you start watering it again, it bounces back." He started crawling. "You were much easier to look after when you stayed where we put you," Parvana told him. They had to watch him carefully, as he put everything he found into his mouth, whether it was good for him or not.

Hassan would allow himself to be fed by anybody, but he clearly prefered Asif. When he got bored with Asif, he crawled around looking for other fun things. He loved to watch the pigeons, and when the children couldn't find him, that's usually where he was.

"Hassan is standing up!" Asif yelled one day. The others came running. Hassan had hauled himself up by holding onto the wires of the pigeon cage. He grinned and laughed as he reached for the pigeons, but when he let go of the cage, he fell back on his rump. He looked surprised, then reached out and hauled himself back up again.

Then one morning, the children couldn't find Hassan. He wasn't at the pigeon cage or inside the house. Parvana got a cold feeling in her stomach.

"He can't be in the mine field!"

"Well, don't just stand there. Run after him!" Asif yelled.

Leila was faster. Hassan had crawled through the little canyon and was right on the edge of the mine field. Leila snatched him up.

"You can't go there," she said, as Hassan screeched. "You're not protected yet." She handed him over to Parvana as he squirmed and fussed.

The children discussed the problem. "We can't let him crawl into the mine field," Parvana said, "but we don't want to chase after him all day, either."

Asif came up with a solution.

"Tie a long rope around his waist. Then he can crawl around without going anywhere he shouldn't." They tried this, and it worked fine.

As long as he had something to lean against, Asif found that he was very good at patching mud walls. He fashioned a device with long boards that let him reach the high spots. Soon the house looked stronger.

Leila and Parvana dug up some wildflowers from the edge of the mine field and replanted them in the yard. Leila edged the little flowerbed with rocks. Parvana remembered the flowers she had once planted in the marketplace in Kabul. She wondered whether they were blooming.

None of the children knew anything about growing vegetables, but when Parvana pulled the weeds and dead plants out of the garden, she found some things growing there already.

"Maybe seeds fell from last year's vegetables," she said to Leila, who was helping her.

"Maybe it's magic," Leila said. "I told you, the ground likes me."

Leila started burying bits of Hassan's food along with hers at the start of each meal. After some prodding, Parvana began to do the same thing. She felt foolish at first, but then it became a habit.

Asif refused. "There's no protection against land mines," he insisted. "You two are idiots."

"Is that how you lost your leg?" Parvana asked. She had never dared ask him before, but if he was willing to tell Leila about his family, maybe he was prepared to talk about his leg, too.

She was wrong.

"No, it wasn't a land mine," he said, glaring at her. "It was...a wolf who ate my leg, but I ate the wolf, so I won that battle."

"You're very brave," Leila said. Asif smiled at her and stuck his thin chest out a little.

Parvana just rolled her eyes.

Every afternoon, Parvana went to a shady spot in the yard and wrote to her friend.

Dear Shauzia:

We patched up the pigeon cage this morning and cleaned it out. I wish we had some vegetable seeds. With all the fertilizer from the pigeons, we could have a wonderful vegetable patch.

Some chickens would be nice, too. Pigeons are good to eat, but I prefer chicken.

Maybe another peddler will get caught in the mine field, a peddler with chickens and seeds and lanterns and lantern oil, and toys for Hassan, books for me, a false leg for Asif, real jewelry for Leila and some new toshaks. Fluffy ones without bugs in them.

Until then, we'll have to make do with what we have.

Parvana read back over what she had written, thinking how lovely it would be to have all those things. Then she realized that for her wishes to come true, some peddler would have to die.

For a moment she wondered what she was becoming. Then she dismissed the question. "I didn't create this world," she said to herself. "I only have to live in it."

FOURTEEN

Leila and Parvana took turns taking care of Grandmother. She didn't need much attention. She just stayed in her corner, eating and sleeping. A few times a day Parvana or Leila would take her a pan, give her some privacy while she used it, and then they would take the pan away again to empty it in the latrine.

At first the children were careful to be quiet around Grandmother, but they soon forgot to worry about her and chattered as much inside the house as they did outside. Sometimes Hassan would use her as a prop when he worked on his standing skills. If Grandmother minded any of this, she gave no sign.

Parvana found some needles and thread in the treasure house.

"Let me fix your dress," she said to Leila. "What you've done is pretty, but I think I can make it even prettier."

Although the dress Parvana made for Leila

had sleeves that weren't even — she wasn't very good at sewing — it did look a little more normal than what Leila had been wearing, and the material she used brought out the blue in the little girl's eyes.

One day, weeks after they had arrived, Parvana decided to wash the dust off the shelves in the little house. She remembered how her mother and Nooria had endlessly washed out the cupboard in the tiny room the family shared in Kabul, using up the water she'd had to walk so far to fetch.

Maybe they could add a room to their Green Valley house, or even two rooms. Her mother, Grandmother and Nooria could sleep in one room. Hassan would make a great little brother for her brother, Ali, and Asif could share a room with them and watch out for them. She could sleep in the third room with her little sister Maryam and Leila. It would be so wonderful to have everyone together.

A pang of missing her family shot through her.

She dropped the cloth back in the bucket and dashed up the hill to the look-out point. Leila was already up there.

"See anything today?"

"I saw some tanks drive by," Leila said, "but I don't think they saw me, because they didn't shoot me."

"The war won't find us here," Parvana said, stroking Leila's hair. "The road is far away. See any mothers yet?"

Leila peered out at the landscape again.

"No, no mothers today."

"Maybe tomorrow," Parvana said.

"Maybe tomorrow."

Parvana squatted down beside her new sister. "If they don't show up soon, I'll have to go looking for them again."

"We could take turns sitting up here," Leila said. "If one of us was always here, they wouldn't be able to slip by without us spotting them."

I have to continue my journey, Parvana thought. She remembered the long months of being hungry and tired, walking through the countryside. She would be alone this time, too. She couldn't ask Asif to go with her. He was making this place his home. And it would be wrong to take Hassan away from where he was fed and happy.

"You're going to stay here forever, aren't you?" Leila asked, entwining her fingers with Parvana's. "We're sisters. You have to stay."

"I'll stay," Parvana said, but she did not say forever. She gave Leila's hand a squeeze, then went back to her house cleaning.

"I will continue my search," she vowed out loud as she finished scrubbing the shelves. "I will. Just...not quite yet."

That decided, she felt much better, and she took a deep, satisfied breath. Then she looked around the tiny one-room house for something else to do.

She had already swept the floor mat with a leafy branch, but she wasn't pleased with the result. It really ought to be taken outside to have the dust beaten out of it. The toshaks should all be aired out, too. Maybe the warm sun would drive the bed bugs and lice out of them.

"Mother wouldn't recognize me," Parvana laughed, "doing housework without being told." She was even wearing girl-clothes all the time again, except when she did nasty cleaning jobs. Her hair was growing back, too. Soon she would be able to tuck bits of it behind her ears.

She pulled two of the three toshaks out of the house and into the yard. Then she bent down, grabbed a corner of the mat and tugged. But the mat wouldn't move.

Grandmother — that was the reason! The mat ran under the toshak where Grandmother crouched.

"You need to be aired out just like the furniture," Parvana said. She laughed at herself. She sounded just like her mother's bossy friend, Mrs. Weera.

Parvana went out into the yard. Leila had come down from the look-out and was hitting one of the toshaks with a stick to beat out the dust and bugs. Asif was keeping Hassan entertained with a piece of wood he moved in the dirt like a toy car. He made car noises that Hassan tried to mimic.

"Can your grandmother walk?" Parvana asked Leila.

"She could before Mother left."

"Let's bring her outside," Parvana said. "It will be good for her, and it will give us a chance to give the inside of the house a good cleaning."

Asif couldn't help much, but he went into

the house with them with Hassan crawling along behind. He liked to try to grab at Asif's crutches as he walked.

Parvana and Leila crouched down in front of the old woman.

"We're going to take you outside now, Grandmother," Leila said.

The woman didn't respond.

"How will we do this?" Leila asked. "We can't carry her."

"Pull her out on the toshak," Asif suggested. As if he could understand, Hassan crawled up onto the mattress beside Grandmother. He giggled.

The girls grabbed the end of the mattress and slowly pulled it across the room and out the door. Parvana saw Grandmother's old thin hands grip the sides of the mattress so she wouldn't fall off, but she made no other movement. Hassan laughed at getting a free ride.

"Let's put her in the sun for awhile," Leila suggested. "If it gets too hot, we can move her into the shade."

Hassan thought the old woman was something to climb on, so Asif led him back to the game they had been playing.

Parvana and Leila brought the floor mat outside, beat the dirt out of it and left it basking in the sun. Then they gave the inside of the house a good hard scrubbing until it smelled much better and looked much brighter.

They brought Grandmother outside every day after that. One afternoon, when they weren't watching Hassan closely enough, he snatched the chador off the old woman's head, tossed it on his own and laughed out loud.

Grandmother crouched down to cover her face. Leila took the chador away from Hassan and was going to give it back to Grandmother when Parvana stopped her. "Let's wash it first."

While it was drying, Leila combed the old woman's long, graying hair with her fingers. Slowly, her body began to unfold, and her face lifted to the sun. Parvana wasn't absolutely certain, but she thought she saw the old woman smile.

Days and weeks went by — golden days full of sun and enough food and lots of happy work. The sores on Leila's face completely healed, Hassan grew strong, and Asif stopped coughing. Often at night they would sit around the cook-fire and tell stories or sing songs. Hassan usually fell asleep in Asif's lap, but sometimes, if Grandmother sat out with them, he would fall asleep against her, and Parvana would see her gently stroke the little boy's hair as he slept.

Dear Shauzia:

On good days, Grandmother sits facing the door when she's inside. Sometimes she has harder days and goes back to facing the wall. I tell her it's okay. I know all about bad days.

No sign of our mothers yet. Leila says it's just a matter of time. I hope Nooria doesn't go all bossy as soon as she gets here. I hope she respects that I found this place before she did, and what I say goes, but that might be too much to hope for.

On very, very good days, Grandmother practices standing up. Her legs are not strong enough yet to hold her up for very long.

Sometimes Hassan tries to stand at the same time. They practice together, and they look so much alike that it really is very funny to watch. Even Asif laughs, although that isn't very fair of me, because he laughs all the time now. We tell Grandmother we're laughing at the baby, but really we're laughing at them both.

"I don't know how to write," Leila said, crouching beside Parvana. "I've never been to school. My mother didn't go. Neither did my grandmother. They wanted to send me, but now there's no school."

"I can teach you how to read and write," Parvana said. Asif was sitting nearby holding Hassan's hands and trying to get him to stand on his own. Parvana saw him raise his head, although he didn't say anything.

"Can you teach Grandmother, too?"

Parvana nodded. "Sure."

"She always wanted to own a book," Leila continued. "She used to tell me that if she had a book, she'd learn to read it, and she would sit and read her book when the work was done for the day. She said it would give her new things to think about, and she'd like that."

Parvana knew at once what to do.

There were two of her father's books left. One was a small book with a paper cover. The other was large with a hard cover. She took the large book inside to Grandmother.

Grandmother was having a bad day. She was back in her usual spot, facing the wall, her head covered over again.

"I have a present for you, Grandmother," Parvana said, sliding the book onto the mattress. She placed the old woman's hand on the book's cover. "It's a book, for your very own. And I will teach you how to read it."

The thin, wrinkled hand slowly stroked the book's cover and thumbed the pages. Parvana was about to go back to Leila when the old woman grabbed her hand and squeezed it.

"You're welcome," Parvana said. She slipped her father's last book into her shoulder bag where she kept her letters to Shauzia.

Her father would be pleased, she thought. And she smiled.

FIFTEEN

The weeks sped by. Parvana knew that time was passing, but she didn't think to keep track of the days. Some days it rained, but most days were sunny. She knew by the coolness of the evenings that the summer was turning into autumn.

"We're down to the last sack of flour," Asif said one morning. He had appointed himself in charge of food supplies. "There's only one full can of cooking oil left, and one and a half sacks of rice."

"Are you sure?" Parvana asked.

Asif just looked at her with disdain before turning his back and walking away.

Parvana climbed up to the look-out point to watch for her mother and think. The breeze at the top of the little hill was chilly.

She tried to figure out how long the food would last. They had apples now, too, but not very many.

"Even if we're very careful, the food won't last the winter," she said to the air. She had been too busy enjoying herself when she should have been worrying about the coming winter.

Leila climbed up the hill and sat down beside her. One of her braids had come loose. Parvana rebraided it as they talked.

"Any mothers yet?" Leila asked.

"Not today."

"Maybe tomorrow."

"We're running out of food," Parvana said, then wished she could snatch the words back. It wasn't right to worry the little girl. But she would have to know soon, wouldn't she?

"Don't worry," Leila said. "The mine field will take care of us."

"I hope it happens soon."

They watched as a group of planes streamed across a corner of the sky. A moment later there was a sound like thunder rumbling in the distance. Then they saw dust rise up from the far hills.

The girls had seen these planes before. They were nothing special.

"Grownups killing each other," Parvana

said, and she turned away to look for her mother in the other direction.

"I kill," Leila said.

Parvana looked at her.

"I kill pigeons," Leila said. "I don't like to do it, but it's not hard. It must be much harder to kill a goat or a donkey. Is it hard to kill a child?" she asked suddenly.

"It should be," Parvana said, "but some people seem to find it awfully easy."

"As easy as killing a pigeon?"

"Easier, I think."

"We eat dead pigeons," Leila said. "What do they do with all the dead children?"

Parvana didn't even try to answer that question. She put her arm around her new little sister, and together they watched the bombs go off, way in the distance.

As the days went by the children saw many more planes in the sky. The sound of explosions went on around them all night, night after night.

"I can't sleep with all that noise," Leila complained. "Don't those grownups know there are children trying to sleep down here?"

"Maybe we should go somewhere else," Asif said.

"Nothing will happen to us here," Parvana said. "Besides, Grandmother can't walk very far yet." The old woman had worked up to taking a few steps in the yard, but she was still very slow.

All night long the sky would rumble like a thunderstorm. The noise stopped in the morning, and the children sometimes stayed in bed until midday, catching up on the sleep they had lost.

In the afternoons, Parvana taught school. Leila was eager to learn, but she found it hard to keep still and silent during lessons. Grandmother sat beside Leila, holding her book and listening. Parvana wasn't sure how much she was learning, but she liked having her there.

"I don't need your stupid school," Asif announced. He took care of Hassan during the lessons, but Parvana noticed they were always close enough to be able to hear what she was saying. Sometimes she saw him trying to draw the letters in the dust with the tip of his crutch, but he always made sure to rub out his efforts afterward.

One afternoon Parvana was teaching Leila how to count using piles of stones. Hassan was standing on Asif's foot, his arms clinging to Asif's leg. Every time Asif took a step, Hassan swung and giggled. Parvana kept frowning at them — the giggling was distracting — but they kept doing it anyway.

Then they heard the sound of an explosion in the field beyond the canyon.

"Did you hear that?" Leila yelled as she jumped to her feet. "I told you the mine field would take care of us!" She sprinted off down the canyon toward the mine field. Parvana followed her.

"Are you two crazy?" Asif hollered. "Get back here!"

Parvana paid no attention to him. Although Leila had a head start, Parvana's legs were longer, and soon she was right behind the little girl. They dashed through the field to the place where the dust was still billowing from the explosion.

"It's a goat!" Leila exclaimed. "The mine only got a part of it. Most of it is still here!"

They each took hold of one of the dead goat's legs and dragged it back across the mine field. Parvana thought again about a spider snatching a fly that flew into its web.

Asif waited for them at the mouth of the canyon. He was waving a crutch and yelling at them.

"You are both idiots! You could have been killed!"

"If you call us idiots, we won't give you any meat for supper," Parvana said. She and Leila laughed as they ducked away from the waving crutch.

They put on their most tattered clothes and got the goat ready for cooking. Asif peeled away the skin and chopped the carcass into pieces. They decided to roast most of the meat and put the smaller bones in a pot to boil for soup.

"Let's all get cleaned and dressed up," Parvana suggested, after the nasty part of the job was done and they had buried the remains outside the canyon. "Let's have a party."

Leila loved the idea and, as suppertime grew near and the smell of the roasting goat filled Green Valley, even Asif got into the spirit of it. He washed and put on clean clothes and got Hassan clean and dressed up as well.

After helping Grandmother clean and change, Parvana scrubbed herself and put on

Leila's mother's blue shalwar kameez. Her hair felt soft from the washing. She shook her head to feel it fluff out around her neck. It really was growing back!

On impulse, she took a flower from the bottle full of wildflowers Leila kept on the windowsill and tucked it behind her ear.

"Oh, Parvana, you look really pretty!" Leila said. "Doesn't she look pretty, Asif?"

Asif looked at Parvana and made throw-up noises. Parvana turned her back on him. She would not let him ruin the party for her.

The roasted goat was delicious. Parvana wasn't sure how long the cooked meat would last without going bad, so everyone ate as much as they could.

There was still a bit of light in the sky. Parvana fetched her shoulder bag from the house. She meant to write to Shauzia about the meal from the mine field, but when she got back to the fire, Leila and Asif were singing. She slung the bag over her shoulder and joined them until the fire burned down into deep red embers.

They were still singing when night came and the bombs started falling again.

The thunder noise was much louder tonight. Parvana could feel the earth vibrate beneath her. She put her arm around Leila. Asif held Hassan in his lap.

Parvana's heart beat hard in her chest as the children kept singing. The louder the bombs, the louder they sang. Parvana was too scared to be able to think of what else to do.

Then a bomb fell right outside Green Valley. The earth shook violently. The noise sounded right through the hands they clamped over their ears. Hassan screamed.

Parvana and Asif moved the younger ones over beside the boulders on the edge of the clearing.

"Grandmother! Come over here!" Leila yelled.

But Grandmother had rolled back up into a ball and covered her head.

Leila tried to go to her but Parvana wouldn't let her. With one hand she held onto Leila. With the other hand she held onto Asif, who shielded Hassan with his body.

Parvana held on tightly as the earth shook more and more. She held on even though Leila writhed and screamed to get to her grandmother.

She was holding on when a bomb fell directly on Green Valley.

Dust, rocks and debris fell on the children's backs. Parvana couldn't tell who was screaming. Maybe it was her.

They clung to each other through the darkness of the night, as the bombs continued to fall all around them.

Silence came with the morning light.

There was a large crater in the yard.

Grandmother was gone. The house was gone.

Green Valley was gone.

SIXTEEN

*D*ear Shauzia:
We're back on the road. It almost feels like we never left. Maybe Green Valley was just a dream. I should stop dreaming. All my dreams turn into garbage.

As hard as it was before, it seems harder this time. It's harder to sleep on the bare ground after months of sleeping on a mattress. It's harder to be hungry after months of eating every day. And it's harder to spend the days wandering after having a home again.

I hope you are living somewhere wonderful. You will have to have a truly spectacular life to make up for the waste mine has become.

Leila didn't want to leave the clearing. She kept saying her mother would come back and not find her. She made me leave a note for her mother. I'm glad Leila can't read much, because I had to put in the note that I have no idea where we are going.

Hassan cries and cries and cries. I felt sad for him at first. Now I just hate the noise.

As if he knew what she was writing, Hassan let out an extra-loud wail.

Parvana threw down her notebook.

"Shut up!" she yelled. "We've tried to help you and we can't, so stop crying!"

"He doesn't understand you," Asif said, taking the baby onto his lap. "He got used to eating, and he's angry at us for not feeding him."

Parvana hated it that Asif was behaving better than she was. She picked up her notebook and put it back in her shoulder bag. Then she noticed that Leila was crying again, too.

"Do you want a reading lesson?" Parvana asked her gently. "My father used to give me lessons when we took breaks."

Leila shook her head and wiped away some of the tears that were rolling down her cheeks.

"I should have gone to Grandmother," she said. "You should have let me go."

Parvana tried to hug the little girl, but Leila pulled out of her grasp. Leila cried quietly — not loud like Hassan — but Parvana was just as tired of hearing it. She walked away and sat down with her back to them. She had no idea what to do.

A row of tanks rolled by in the distance, and two planes flew in the sky above her, although she didn't see any bombs falling from them. Parvana didn't pay them any attention. Tanks were normal. Bombs were normal. Why couldn't eating be normal?

They had salvaged what they could after the house was bombed. There was a bit of rice spilled on the ground. They picked it out of the dirt grain by grain. There wasn't enough water to cook the rice, and no cook-pot, so the children had to chew the rice kernels raw.

The food and water lasted them for a few days. Then it ran out. That was two days ago. It was longer for Hassan, because he couldn't chew raw rice.

Their only blanket was the blanket shawl Asif had been wearing around his shoulders when the bomb hit. That, plus Parvana's shoulder bag, was all they had. Hassan had no change of clothing, and already he stank again.

Parvana carried him most of the time. He wanted to be crawling, so he kicked and fussed whenever he was carried. He stank, so Parvana stank. Her once beautiful light blue clothes were now a stinking mess.

"We're worse off than we were before," Parvana said to the air. To top it off, she was dressed in girl clothes. Whatever she did now, she'd have to do it as a girl — a girl who was getting to be too old to be uncovered in public, according to the Taliban. She didn't even have a head covering. She had been enjoying her hair too much on the night of the party to cover it up.

"Are you just going to sit there like an idiot?" Asif yelled. He had to yell loudly to make his voice heard over Hassan's screeching.

She sat with her back to them for awhile longer, then got to her feet. She went back to the others, lifted Hassan, helped Asif stand up, and gently nudged Leila.

"Let's go," she said.

The children started walking again, because there was nothing else to do.

Toward the middle of the afternoon, Asif let out a shout. "There's a stream!"

Parvana looked where he was pointing. He was right. It wasn't much of a stream, but at least it was wet.

"We should boil it first," Parvana said, but Asif and Leila were already scooping water into their mouths. Parvana realized she was being a fool. There was no way they could boil water. If they got sick, they got sick. It was better than dying of thirst.

She made a cup with her hands and drank deeply. The water was muddy, but that didn't matter. She scooped up water for Hassan to drink, too.

She started to undress the baby.

"What are you doing?" Asif asked.

"I'm going to wash him and wash his clothes. In case you haven't noticed, he stinks."

"I thought that was you."

Parvana snatched the blanket shawl from Asif's shoulders. "To keep the baby warm," she said. For a moment she hoped Hassan would wet the blanket — it would serve Asif right — but quickly changed her mind when she remembered that they all had to sleep under that blanket.

They stayed by the stream for the rest of the day, drinking water whenever their bellies felt empty again.

"Hassan's clothes aren't dry," Leila said as night fell. "We can't dress him in wet clothes. He'll catch cold. You should have waited until tomorrow to wash his clothes."

Asif took off his shirt and wrapped it around the baby. Parvana could feel Asif shivering all night long.

The next morning was chilly. Hassan had messed Asif's shirt, so Parvana had to wash it out. Asif kept the blanket around his shoulders, while he waited for his shirt to dry, but it took too long in the cold air. He eventually put it back on while it was still wet.

"You don't know where we are, do you?" Asif accused Parvana, as his thin body cringed at the touch of the cold, wet cloth on his skin.

"No, I don't," Parvana said, too tired to try to think up something reassuring.

"Do you know where we're going?"

"We're going to find food," Parvana replied. "Now you know as much as I do, and if you don't like it, you're free to go off on your own."

"Don't think I won't do that," Asif grumbled.

"Is there any food in your bag?" Leila asked.

"No, of course not."

"Why don't you check?" Leila suggested. "Maybe there's something in there you forgot."

"I wouldn't forget about food. There's no food in my bag."

"Then why don't you check?" Asif said. "If you don't check, it's because you're hiding something. You probably have all kinds of food in there that you eat when we're asleep."

Parvana let out a deep, annoyed breath and dumped the contents of her shoulder bag onto the ground so everyone could see.

"Matches, notebook full of letters to my friend, pens, my mother's magazine, book." She touched each item as she identified it. "No food."

"What is that book?" Leila asked.

Parvana picked up the small book with the paper cover. "It's in English," she said, pointing at the letters.

"You know some English," Leila urged. "Tell us what it says."

Parvana's English was not very good, and she had to concentrate, which was hard. Her brain had that sluggish feeling it always got when she was hungry. She sounded out the words the way her father had taught her, then translated them.

"To Kill a Mockingbird," she said slowly.

"What's a mockingbird?" Asif asked.

Parvana didn't know. "It's like a ... a chicken," she said. "This book is about killing chickens."

"That's dumb," Asif said. "Why would anyone write a whole book about killing chickens?"

"There are lots of ways to kill a pigeon," Leila said. "Maybe there are lots of ways to kill a chicken. Maybe it's a book that tells us the *best* way to kill a chicken. Or maybe it's about what to do with a chicken once it's been killed. You know, different ways to cook it."

"I like it cooked over the fire the best," Asif said. "Remember the chicken we stole?" he asked Parvana. "That was delicious."

Parvana agreed. That had been a particularly good meal.

"My mother used to make a stew with chicken," she said. "She made it for my birthday once, back when we lived in a whole house with lots of rooms. We had a party. Even Nooria was nice that day." More out of habit than hope, Parvana quickly looked around in case her mother was coming.

"Do you suppose the book tastes like chicken?" Leila asked.

"No, I wouldn't think so," Parvana said.

"It probably does," Asif said. "She's probably keeping it all for herself. She's mean like that."

"Parvana's not mean," Leila insisted, which was the first nice thing she had said about Parvana since the bombing. "If that book was good to eat, she'd share it with us."

"She's meaner than an old goat," Asif insisted.

"Oh, here, see for yourselves!" Parvana tore some pages out of the mockingbird book and handed them out.

"What about you?" Leila asked. "You must be hungry, too."

Parvana tore a page out for herself and one for Hassan, but Hassan was getting that floppy-baby look again and wasn't interested.

"What are we waiting for?" Parvana asked. She bit into the page, tearing a chunk off with her teeth. The others did the same.

The book didn't taste like chicken. It didn't taste like anything, but it was something to chew on, and each child ate another page after they finished the first.

"Where do we go from here?" Asif asked.

"Someone else decide," Parvana said, stretching out on the ground. "I'm tired of being the leader."

"If it doesn't matter where we go, why don't we follow the stream?" Leila suggested. "At least we'll have something to drink that way."

Parvana sat up and looked at the girl with admiration. "At least one of us is thinking," she said.

"I was just going to suggest that," Asif insisted.

The children looked up and down the stream. "There are some trees up this way," Asif said. "Maybe we'll find something to eat."

It was good to have a plan, even a small one, so the children headed off again.

SEVENTEEN

The bombing continued night after night. Sometimes it was far away, sometimes a little closer, but always, when darkness fell, thunder sounds rolled across the sky.

"Who is under the bombs?" Leila asked one night. All four children were huddled together under the one blanket. The two youngest ones were in the middle where it was warmer. Parvana had the old rocks-in-the-back problem, but moving herself would have meant moving all four of them. Asif and Hassan were sleeping.

"Parvana, who's under the bombs?" Leila asked again.

"I don't know," Parvana whispered back. "People like us, I guess."

"Why do the bombs want to kill them?"

"Bombs are just machines," Parvana said. "They don't know who they kill."

"Who does?"

Parvana wasn't sure. "Since the bombs come from airplanes, someone must have put them there, but I don't know who, or why they want to kill the people they're killing tonight."

"Why did they want to kill Grandmother? She never knew anyone who put things on planes, so how would they even know her to kill her?"

"I don't know," Parvana said. She took hold of Leila's hand under the blanket. "We're sisters, right?"

"Yes, we're sisters."

"As your big sister, it's my job to protect you," she said. "That's why I had to keep you from going to your grandmother that night. Do you understand?"

"I understand," Leila said. "You were doing your job. I was angry at you, but I'm not any more."

"When my father died, it made me feel better to remember things about him. Why don't you tell me something you remember about your grandmother?"

"She used to sing," Leila said, after thinking for a moment. "She taught me a song about a bird. Would you like to hear it?"

Parvana said she would. Leila sang the song.

"It's like she's still here when I remember her like that," she said. "Do you think she's happy now? What do you think she's doing?"

"I think people get to do what they want after they die," Parvana said. "Your grandmother wanted to read, so she's probably sitting in the warm sun surrounded by books, reading and smiling."

"I'd like to be surrounded by pretty things," Leila said.

"You *are* a pretty thing," Parvana told her.

"So are you. We're both pretty things," Leila giggled.

"Can't you girls ever stop talking?" Asif complained. He turned his back to them, yanking the blanket with him.

Parvana didn't yank it back. Asif's cough had returned. She moved in closer to Leila for warmth against the cold, dark night.

For the next few days the children stuck close to the stream as it got thinner and thinner. The water made them all sick, but they kept drinking it anyway. They ate leaves and grass and some more pages from the mockingbird book.

Hassan stopped crying. He barely whimpered now, and he wouldn't eat any of the leaves they tried to put in his mouth. He didn't turn his head away or spit them out. They would just fall from his lips because he couldn't hold them there.

The ground by the stream was rocky and hard to walk on. They had to move slowly so Asif wouldn't fall. Sometimes they saw people in the distance, but they had no energy to rush over to them for help, and their voices would not carry that far.

They had been walking for four days when Leila suddenly spotted something up ahead.

"Look," she said.

Parvana had been keeping her eyes on the ground, looking for the smoothest way for Asif's crutches. She looked up. Not too far in front of them were some people on a cart. They didn't appear to be soldiers.

"Maybe they'll give us a ride," Parvana said.

"I'll run ahead and see," Leila said.

As they got closer, Parvana could see a woman in a burqa and children in the cart, and a man standing beside it.

They caught up with Leila. She looked up at

them and shook her head, then nodded at the broken cart wheel.

"We cannot help you," the man said. "We cannot even help ourselves."

"Can you at least give us food for the baby?" Parvana asked, holding Hassan out to show them what bad shape he was in.

The woman in the cart uncovered the baby she was carrying. It looked like Hassan. Parvana noticed the other children also had dull eyes and sores on their faces like Leila used to have.

"Our baby will soon die," the man said. "Yours will, too."

"He won't," Asif said.

The man went on as if Asif hadn't spoken.

"I am a farmer, but the bombs made holes in my land. There has been so little rain — nothing to help the land recover from the bombs. This stream used to be a river. I caught fish here as a boy. The water was good to drink. Now there are only rocks. Can we drink rocks? Can we eat rocks?" He touched the broken cart wheel gently, too worn out for anger.

"Where do we go now?" Parvana asked him.

"We have heard there is a camp in that direction." He pointed across the river. "I don't know exactly where. Go that way. You will meet others. There are many people trying to get away from the bombing."

Parvana reached out and took hold of the hand of the woman under the burqa. The woman squeezed her hand back. Then the children went on their way.

"This must be the river bank," Parvana said when they got to the edge of the rocky surface. "See where the water cut through the soil?"

The river bank was steep. Asif had to go up backwards on his bottom while Leila carried his crutches. It was slow going, and the effort made him cough a lot. They had to rest before they could go on.

"I smell smoke," Leila said later that afternoon. "Maybe there are people ahead cooking supper. Maybe they have lots of food and will share some with us."

"I don't think anyone around here has lots of food," Parvana said. She could smell the smoke, too. "But we might as well go and see."

They headed toward the smell. They found it at the bottom of a small hill.

The children stood on the hill and looked down at a forest of blackened trees. Some of them were still smoking.

"What is it?" Leila asked.

"It's an orchard," Asif said. "See how the trees are in rows? It's a place to grow fruit."

The trees would grow nothing now.

"My uncle had an orchard," Asif said. "He grew peaches, mostly, and rows of berry bushes. He accused me of stealing berries from him. Is it stealing to take food when you're hungry? I worked and worked for him, and he didn't give me enough food."

"Is that why he whipped you?" Parvana asked. If Asif wanted to talk, she wanted to listen.

"He never told me why he whipped me. I don't think he needed a reason. When he caught me eating the berries, he locked me in the shed. He said he was going to get the Taliban to cut off my hands."

"How did you get out?"

"Crutches are good for breaking locks," Asif said. Then he headed down the hill into the burnt-out orchard. The others followed him. They soon came across bomb craters in the ground.

Parvana didn't like it in the orchard. She kept thinking she saw things moving among the silent black tree trunks. She wondered what sort of trees they had been. Peach? Apricot? Cherry?

There were no birds singing. That's why it was so quiet.

"Leila, teach us the bird song your grand-mother sang to you."

"I don't feel like singing."

"But I do. It will help me to not be afraid."

Leila taught them the song. They sang it until they were out of the orchard. It was a place of death, and Parvana was glad to leave it behind.

EIGHTEEN

Dear Shauzia:
The man with the broken cart was right. We see a lot of people now, traveling like we are. We beg from everyone we see. We even beg from people who are trying to beg from us. Most people don't have anything. If they do, they share it with us — sometimes just a mouthful, but it helps us stay alive another day.

People keep telling us to take Hassan to a doctor, but we don't know any doctors, and we have no money to pay for one.

I wonder if that man ever got his cart out of the river bed. I wonder if their baby will live.

I wonder if we will live.

The children followed a road now, going in the same direction as the other travelers. Sometimes a truck full of soldiers passed them. Once a short line of tanks rumbled by, and everyone had to get off the road to let them pass. Parvana remembered the tank the children had played on in the village where her father died. She wondered if children would play on these tanks one day.

Later they heard the tanks shooting at something.

The planes were bombing in the daytime now, as well as at night. Some of the bombs were so loud that the noise knocked the children to the ground. Asif cut his face when he fell against some rocks. A lot of blood ran from his forehead. He had to keep wiping the cut with his blanket, because they had no bandages.

More bombs fell. One exploded just ahead of them. People scattered, huddling in clumps on each side of the road.

"Get down!" people shouted. "Take cover!"

Parvana ran with the baby to the side of the road. Asif was close behind her. She was face down in the dirt, dust and rocks billowing around her, when she realized Leila wasn't with her.

She peered out through the falling rubble and saw Leila still standing in the road. The little girl had her hands cupped over her mouth, and she was shouting something into the sky.

Parvana slid Hassan over to Asif and ran into the road. As she got closer, she could hear what Leila was saying.

"Stop!" Leila shouted at the airplanes. "Don't do this any more!"

The airplanes ignored her. The bombs kept falling.

Parvana would never know how she found the strength. She picked Leila up and ran with her to the side of the road, then lay on top of her to keep her from rushing out again. Her free hand found Asif's. They stayed like that until the planes finished their bombing.

When everything was quiet except for the crying of people who had lost loved ones, and the screaming of those who had been injured, the children got up and started walking again. They couldn't help anyone, and no one could help them.

Parvana saw a man cradling a dead boy, an injured woman with her burqa flipped back from her face, gasping for air, a child shaking a woman on the ground who was not responding.

The children had to walk around dead pack animals and broken wagons and bits of people's belongings scattered in the road — shoes, pots, a green water jug, a broken shovel. There was smoke and the smell of gasoline, and the sounds of agony and madness. It all made Parvana feel as if she were walking through a wide-awake nightmare.

"Do you suppose we're all dead?" Asif asked.

Parvana didn't even try to answer. She just kept walking.

The children walked for the rest of the day. They were just four more bodies in a long line of people moving forward only because there was nothing to go back to.

"I don't even feel like me any more," Parvana said, talking more to herself than to anyone else. "The part of me that's me is gone. I'm just part of this line of people. There's no me left. I'm nothing."

"You're not nothing," Asif said.

Parvana stopped walking and looked at him.

"You're not nothing," he said again. Then he grinned a little. "You're an idiot. That's not nothing."

Before he could stop her, Parvana wrapped his frail body in a gigantic hug. To her great surprise, he hugged her back before pushing her away with mock disgust.

They kept walking.

As the sky grew darker, mountains and hills became balls of fire and pillars of smoke from the bombs dropped on them. Parvana's eyes stung from the thick smoke in the air. Her throat, already parched from thirst, burned when she tried to swallow.

Night was almost upon them when they reached the top of a small ridge and looked down.

Spread out below them, as far as they could see, was a mass of tents and people.

Parvana knew what they were looking at. She had stayed in a place much like it, with her father, last winter.

It was a camp for Internally Displaced Persons. It was a camp for internal refugees.

It was a home for four tired and hungry children.

NINETEEN

"We have hundreds of people a day flooding in here," the nurse in the Red Crescent Clinic said to Parvana and the others as she took charge of Hassan. "Things were bad enough already. Then someone dropped a bomb on our supply depot. Tents, blankets, food and medicine all went up in smoke before — "

"Will Hassan be all right?" Asif asked.

The nurse had Hassan stripped, washed and diapered with a few quick, practiced movements.

"He's suffering from severe malnutrition and dehydration," she said, putting a needle into Hassan's arm and taping it down.

"What does that mean?" Asif asked.

"It means he's hungry and thirsty," the nurse said.

"I *know* that," Asif almost yelled. "I asked you if he's going to be all right."

"We'll do the best we can," she said, and she began to head off to another patient.

"That's no answer." Asif stuck out his crutch to block her way, and for once Parvana was glad for his rudeness.

The nurse stopped and turned around.

"He's in very bad shape," she said. "I don't know if he'll be all right or not. I've seen sick babies like him recover, though, so don't lose hope. Now, I'm sorry, but you'll have to leave."

Asif lowered himself to the floor beside Hassan's crib. Parvana and Leila sat down beside Asif.

"Where's the rest of your family?" the nurse asked.

"We're it," Parvana said.

The nurse nodded. "Don't get in the way," she said, but gently.

The clinic was just a big tent. They had stood in line for hours to get in. From her spot on the floor, Parvana couldn't see much of what was going on, but she could hear the moans and the weeping, and the sounds from the camp that filtered in under the tent canvas.

Asif and Leila stretched out on the floor under Hassan's crib and were soon asleep, but

Parvana was quite content to sit. She felt as though she could sit for the rest of her life.

The nurse came back after awhile. "Here's another blanket for you. Don't tell anyone you got it here. There aren't enough to go around, and we don't want a riot on our hands." She also gave Parvana some bread and mugs of tea. "You won't be able to stay here all the time," she said, "but you can for now."

For now sounded fine to Parvana. "You're not Afghan," she said to the nurse, who spoke Dari with a foreign accent.

"I am from France," the nurse said. "I am here in Afghanistan with a French relief agency."

"Do you know the fields of purple flowers?" Parvana asked, so excited that she gripped the nurse's arm. "My friend Shauzia is going there. Do they really exist?"

"Yes, I have seen the fields," the nurse said. "The flowers are called lavender. They are made into perfume. Your friend picked a beautiful spot to go to. Now, drink your tea while it's hot. Wake up your brother and sister. They should have a hot drink. They can sleep later."

Parvana woke them up. They drank the tea and went back to sleep.

Parvana spent the night hovering between sleeping and waking. She would start to drift off, then bombs would explode in the distance. Or she would start to dream that they were still walking, walking, walking, and she would wake up again. Every time she did, she checked on Hassan. He looked so small in the crib with a tube sticking out of him. Sometimes when she got up, Asif was already standing there watching the baby.

After a couple of days, the hospital was so crowded that the nurse had to ask the children to leave.

"I'm sure we can find some families who will take you in with them."

"We'll stay just outside the clinic," Parvana said. "We want to stay near our brother."

The nurse gave them a letter. "The World Food Programme has set up a bakery on the other side of the camp," she said. "Give them this letter, and you'll be able to get some bread every day... well, almost every day. I'll get food to you when I can, but it won't be very much or very often."

As a final parting gift, she also gave them a piece of plastic sheeting. Parvana was grateful. She knew how to build a shelter with that.

Outside the clinic, Parvana draped the plastic against the barrier separating the clinic from the rest of the camp. She made a little tent, with enough plastic left over to line the floor.

"We've only been here a few days, and already we have food, shelter and an extra blanket, and Hassan has seen a nurse," Parvana said, forcing her voice to sound cheerful.

"I don't like it here," Leila said. "It's noisy and crowded and it smells bad. Can't we go back to Green Valley? Maybe Grandmother is all right now. Maybe she's sitting on top of the hill waiting for us to come home."

"We're here for the winter," Parvana said firmly. She didn't remind Leila that Grandmother was dead. "We're a family. We stick together. I'm the oldest, so you have to do what I say."

She didn't add that her legs had no more steps in them. As bad as this place was, at least it was somewhere. There were grownups around, and the possibility of regular food. Besides, she wouldn't know where to go from here.

"I'll go and get our bread," Asif offered. He was already lying down in the lean-to, coughing. Both he and Leila were coughing all the time now.

"No, it's all right, I'll go," Parvana said.

She didn't want to go. She didn't want to wade into the sea of desperate people. She knew from her experience at the other camps that going for bread or anything else meant standing in line for hours. She couldn't let Asif do it.

"We need you here to guard our belongings," she told him. To Leila, she said, "You should stay here, too, so that one of you can sleep while the other stands guard."

She told them not to expect her back until the end of the day. Then she put her bag over her shoulder and headed off in the direction the nurse had shown them.

Parvana's days fell into a pattern. She began to move through them as though she were dreaming.

Dear Shauzia:
I can't sleep at night. I doze off for a bit, then Asif coughs, or Leila coughs, or they cry

out in nightmares, or the neighbors yell, and I wake up again. I can't sleep during the day because I have to spend my time standing in lines.

Often my time in lines is wasted. Three times I've lined up for bread only to have the bakery run out before I got there.

Two days ago there was a rumor that some-one was in the camp to choose people to go to Canada. I stood in that line all day, but nothing happened. The line fell apart, and I never found out if the Canada people were really here or not. Either way, I missed lining up for bread that day.

When we first set up our lean-to we were alone on that patch of ground. By the end of the day, when I got back with our bread, there was barely an inch of bare ground around our shelter. I couldn't find our place at first, and ran around in a panic before finally getting home.

Asif's cough is worse. Leila's cough is worse, and we are very cold at night. Hassan is getting better, though. Asif goes to see him every day, leaving Leila to guard our few things. He said yesterday that Hassan was able to grip his fingers, and that he laughed when Asif made *funny faces. He said there is another baby sleeping on a mat under Hassan's crib, so the nurse wasn't lying when she said there was no room for us.*

Everywhere I go, I look for my mother. I should do a proper search, tent to tent, but I spend all my time standing in lines. I'm not even going to hope that I'll find her. Hope is a waste of time.

The nurse told me the purple fields of France really do exist. I hope you're there. I wish I was.

Parvana put her notebook away and shuffled forward a few inches with the rest of the line. She really should be more grateful, she thought. After all, they weren't alone any more, and a proper adult was caring for Hassan. She tried to make herself feel grateful as she stared out over the tents made of rags, stretching all the way to the horizon.

"Excuse me, what is this line for?" a boy asked her.

For a long moment Parvana couldn't remember. She had been standing in the line for such a long time. "Water," she recalled, and held up the empty cooking oil can she had begged from someone else.

Eventually it was her turn at the water truck, and she lugged the full can back to the lean-to.

The bombing was still going on, and refugees kept pushing their way into the camp, squeezing into every square inch of land.

"Why do they have to squash in here?" Parvana complained, as new arrivals threatened to take over the children's lean-to. "There's a whole field on the other side of the clinic. Why don't they go there?"

"It's a mine field," Asif said.

"How do you know?"

He looked at her with his usual scorn. "I know lots of things you don't."

Parvana felt as if she were back in the tiny one-room apartment she had shared with her family in Kabul. Whenever she got angry with Nooria, there was nowhere to go to get away from her. Now with all the bare ground being taken up with tents and shelters, there was nowhere to go to get away from Asif.

She looked out the flap of the lean-to. Inches away was the neighbor's tent. The man and his wife were arguing loudly in a language Parvana didn't understand.

Is this it? she wondered. Have I come so far, just to be here? Is this really my life?

TWENTY

Weeks went by. The weather grew colder. There were days without any bread because a convoy of food trucks had been bombed.

"Maybe the mine field will give us something to eat," Leila said.

"Oh, sure, and what will we cook it with," Parvana said roughly. "Stop dreaming and grow up."

Leila started to cry. Parvana left her alone in the tent. Asif was visiting Hassan, who was much better but was being kept in the clinic because it was warmer there. Parvana was glad she didn't have to worry about him.

She stomped between the tents, pretending to look for her mother, but really just trying to get rid of her anger.

The camp stank of unwashed bodies. There was no place to wash, and it was too cold to get wet, anyway. Parvana didn't have a sweater or a shawl, and the cold made her mood worse.

"Cover up!" a man spat at her. "You are a woman. You should cover up!"

Mind your own business, Parvana thought. He wasn't the first man in the camp to say that to her. She would cover up if she had something to cover up with, preferably something warm. She changed direction and walked away from him.

Most of the women stayed inside the tents. The men and boys stood outside wherever there was room to stand, watching and waiting because there was nothing else to do. Everywhere Parvana went she heard coughing and crying, saw children with ugly sores and runny noses, saw people without limbs and people who seemed to have lost their minds. Some of these people talked to themselves. Some of them did a strange dance, rocking and weeping.

Even after being there for weeks, Parvana hadn't seen the whole camp. Maybe it didn't end. Maybe it just went on and on — an endless sea of crying, stinking, hungry people.

A man walked by carrying a baby.

"Someone please buy my baby so I can feed my family," he pleaded. "My other children are starving. Someone please buy my baby!"

A loud, desperate cry reached Parvana's ears, and she realized it was coming from her own mouth.

A woman in a burqa, her face hidden, came up to Parvana and put her arms around her. She spoke softly in Pashtu. Parvana couldn't understand the words, but she leaned against the woman's comforting shoulders, returning the hug. Then the woman hurried off to catch up with her husband.

Nothing had changed, but Parvana suddenly felt calmer and stronger. She went back to the lean-to to apologize to Leila and pass the hug along.

Later that day, they heard a plane overhead.

"It's going to bomb us!" Leila cried, hiding herself under a blanket.

"It doesn't sound like a bombing plane," Asif said. "Let's go and see."

He and Parvana left the lean-to. A lot of little yellow things were falling from the sky.

"Leila, come out and see," Parvana called,

as one fell not far from where they were standing. "It's all right. There's no bomb."

The people in the camp stared at the bright yellow package for a long minute, wondering if it would explode. A teenaged boy finally walked right up to it, kicked it a bit and then picked it up. He turned it around in his hands and tore open the yellow plastic covering.

"It's food!" he exclaimed. Then he slammed the parcel close to his chest and ran off.

Food! Parvana could see a few other parcels on the ground, and she ran toward them, but so did a lot of other people. Fights broke out as a hundred people dived for one package. Parvana was jostled by the crowd. She kept a firm grip on Leila and Asif.

"We might as well go back to our lean-to," she told them. "There's nothing for us here."

"There's lots more parcels over there," Leila said, pointing toward the mine field. "They look like flowers."

Parvana looked. The field was dotted with bright yellow.

The children were jostled again as the frustrated crowd surged on the edge of the mine field. Parvana and the others were pushed near the front of the flimsy barrier that separated the safe place from the dangerous place.

"Get back!" Some men with sticks tried to bring order. "Stay out of the field! It's dangerous!"

But people kept pushing.

"We need that food!"

"My family is starving!"

Parvana heard bits of cries from others, all saying the same thing.

Parvana felt a tug on her arm. She bent down.

"I can get the food parcels," Leila said into Parvana's ear. "The land mines won't hurt me."

"You stay with me." People kept shoving and shouting around them. "Do you hear me?" Parvana yelled at Leila. "You stay with me."

"I'll be right back," Leila said, and she darted away.

Parvana reached through the crowd and grabbed Leila's arm. She held on, even though the little girl kept pulling to get away.

"We should get Leila out of here before she does something stupid," Parvana shouted to Asif, but her words were lost in the noise of the mob.

Asif shook his head. He couldn't hear her.

Parvana took a deep breath and was just about to shout her message out again when there was an explosion in the mine field.

Horrified, Parvana gave a great yank on the arm she was clutching, and a child came crashing against her. Parvana stared at the girl in shock.

It was not Leila.

"Leila!" she screamed, pushing her way to the barrier. She saw her sister lying in a heap on the mine field.

The crowd was now silent. Parvana could hear Leila moaning.

"She's still alive!" Parvana cried. "We have to go and get her!"

"We must wait until the mine-clearing team gets here," one of the men guarding the field told her.

"When will that be?"

"We expected them two days ago."

"I have to go and get her!" Parvana started to duck under the string barrier. The guard grabbed her around the waist and held her back.

"You cannot help her! You, too, will be killed."

"She's our sister!" Asif started hitting the man with his crutch. "Let her go!"

When the guard raised his arms to protect himself from Asif's crutch, Parvana broke away and slipped under the barrier.

She didn't think about the mines planted in the ground. She didn't think about the crowd yelling at her from behind the barrier. All she could think of was Leila.

She finally reached the little girl. Leila was covered with blood. The mine had damaged her belly as well as her legs. She looked up at Parvana and whimpered.

Parvana knelt down beside her and stroked her hair. "Don't be afraid, little sister," Parvana said. Then she gathered Leila up in her arms and walked back across the mine field to the camp.

Their nurse friend was waiting for them at the barrier. People helped Parvana put Leila gently on the ground. Parvana sat down and held Leila's head in her lap. She was dimly aware of Asif kneeling beside her, and of the nurse trying to help.

Leila was trying to say something. Parvana leaned down so she could hear.

The little girl's voice was thin with pain. "They were so pretty," she said. And then she died.

A great deal of activity began to swirl around Parvana, but none of it touched her. She knew Asif was crying beside her. She knew the crowd was talking and that people were pushing in to see what had happened, but the grief inside Parvana was a solid blackness that kept everything away. She kept her head down, looking into Leila's face. She closed Leila's eyes and smoothed down her hair.

"Another dead child!" a woman cried out. "How many dead Afghan children does the world need? Why is the world so hungry for the lives of our children?"

The woman knelt beside Leila's body.

"Whose child is this?" she asked.

"She is the sister of these two children," someone said.

"Where are her parents? Does she have parents? What have we come to, that a girl can die without her mother?"

Something in the woman's voice reached through Parvana's blackness.

Parvana raised her head. The woman was

wearing a burqa. Parvana reached out her hand and raised the front of the burqa.

Her mother's face looked back at her.

Parvana started to cry. She cried and cried and did not think she ever would be able to stop.

TWENTY-ONE

*D*ear Shauzia:
*I'm writing this letter while I sit at the
edge of another cemetery. It's the only quiet
place in the camp. I'm wearing a warm sweater
Mother found for me.*

*We buried Leila yesterday. I put rocks
around her grave, just like I put them around
my father's grave so long ago.*

*It's not the same, though. I'm not alone this
time. I have my old family — Mother, Nooria
and my little sister Maryam. And I have my
new family — my two brothers, Hassan and
Asif.*

*My baby brother Ali died last winter. Mother
thinks he died of pneumonia, but she's not sure.
There was no doctor around at the time.*

*I told them how Father died. My mother
says it wasn't my fault.*

*There's a lot I haven't told her yet, but
there's time. Our stories can wait.*

*It was pure chance that we found each other
again. Mother's tent is on the far side of the
camp. She was at the clinic with a neighbor
woman who was too shy to go by herself to see
the nurse. When she heard the explosion, she
came running out.*

*I would have found her eventually, though.
It just would have taken me awhile.*

*She and Nooria are part of a women's orga-
nization in the camp. The Taliban are busy
fighting the war so they don't bother women in
the camp very much.*

*The women's organization runs a small
school and tries to match up people who need
things with the things that they need. Mother
said Nooria is especially good at this. I can see
how she would be. She'd be good at anything
that allows her to boss people around.*

*She hasn't been bossy to me yet, but just
wait. A mean old nanny goat doesn't change
into a dove just because a little time has passed.*

*It's wonderful to be complaining about
Nooria again! It makes me feel all warm inside,
like there is at least something normal in the
world.*

I gave mother the women's magazine I'd

carried all the way from Kabul. She was very happy to see it. She's going to pass it around to other women in the camp to cheer them up.

We hear a lot of rumors. Some people say the Americans are doing the bombing. Some people say the Taliban have left Kabul. People say a lot of things. They even say that someone sitting comfortably in one city can press a button and destroy another city, but I know that can't be true.

"Writing another letter to your friend?" Asif hobbled over and eased himself down to the ground beside her.

Parvana didn't answer him, hoping he'd take the hint and leave her in peace.

"I'm surprised you even have a friend," Asif said. "You probably made her up. You're probably writing all those letters to yourself."

"Oh, go away," Parvana said.

Asif, of course, stayed where he was. He gave her a few moments of silence and then said, "I've just been talking with your mother. I talked with your sisters, too. They're both much prettier than you are. I don't think you're even from the same family."

"You and Nooria should get along well," said Parvana. "You're both unbearable."

"You're probably going to stay here with your family now, aren't you?"

"Of course I am. Why wouldn't I?"

"Well, if you think I'm going to stay with you and them, you can forget it."

Here we go again, thought Parvana. "I don't recall asking you to stay."

"I mean, your sisters are pretty, and your mother is nice, but deep down, they're probably all as crazy as you are."

"Probably."

Asif was quiet again for a moment. Parvana knew what was coming. She waited.

"You probably want me to go," he said. "Why don't you just admit it?"

"I want you to go."

"You'd probably hate it if I stayed."

"Yes, I would."

"All right then," said Asif. "I'll stay. Just to annoy you."

Parvana smiled and turned back to her letter.

It's been a long journey, and it's not over yet. I know I won't be living in this camp for the rest of my life, but where will I go? I don't know.

What will happen to us now? Will we be hit by a bomb? Will the Taliban come here and kill us because they are angry at being made to leave Kabul? Will we be buried under the snow when it comes and disappear forever?

These are all worries for tomorrow. For today, my mother is here, and my sisters, and my new brothers.

I hope you are in France. I hope you are warm and your stomach is full and you are surrounded by purple flowers. I hope you are happy and not too lonely.

One way or another, I'll get to France, and I'll be waiting for you at the top of the Eiffel Tower, less than twenty years from now.

Until then, I remain,
Your very best friend,
Parvana.

Afghanistan is a small country in central Asia. It contains the Hindu Kush mountain range, fast-flowing rivers and golden deserts. Its fertile valleys once produced an abundance of fruit, wheat and vegetables. Conquerors and explorers throughout history have seen Afghanistan as a gateway to the Far East.

Afghanistan has been at war since 1978, when American-backed fighters opposed the Soviet-backed government. In 1980, the Soviet Union invaded Afghanistan, and the war escalated, with both sides bombing and killing with modern weapons.

After the Soviets left in 1989, a civil war erupted, as various groups fought for control of the country. Millions of Afghans became refugees, and some still live in huge camps in Pakistan, Iran and Russia. Many people have spent their whole lives in these camps. Millions have been killed, maimed or blinded.

The Taliban militia, an Afghan army, took control of the capital city of Kabul in September, 1996. They imposed extremely restrictive laws on girls and women. Schools for girls were closed down, women were no longer allowed to hold jobs, and strict dress codes were enforced. Books were burned, televisions smashed, and music in any form was forbidden. The Taliban massacred thousands of their opponents, many of them civilians, and put others in prison. Some people simply disappeared, and their families may never know what happened to them.

Although the Taliban is no longer in power in Afghanistan, more than twenty years of war have left the country in terrible shape. Bridges, roads and electrical plants have been destroyed. Few people in Afghanistan have clean water to drink. All the armies put land mines in farmers' fields, making it impossible to grow food there. As a result, many people die of hunger or from diseases caused by poor nutrition.

The greatest sign of hope for Afghanistan is that the schools have reopened, and all children — boys and girls — now have a chance to get an education. The terrible poverty and destruction in the country means they need help from people around the world to build schools and provide basic supplies. With that help, they can rebuild their lives, and start to hope again.

Deborah Ellis
October, 2002

bolani – A kind of dumpling.

burqa – A long, tent-like garment worn by women. It covers the entire body and even has a narrow mesh screen over the eyes.

chador – A piece of cloth worn by women and girls to cover their hair and shoulders.

Dari – One of the two main languages spoken in Afghanistan.

jenazah – A Muslim prayer for the dead.

land mine – A bomb planted in the ground, which explodes if it is stepped on.

mullah – A religious expert and teacher of Islam.

nan – Afghan bread. It can be flat, long and/or round.

Pashtu – One of the two main languages spoken in Afghanistan.

pilaf – A rice dish that usually contains vegetables, meat and spices.

Ramadan – A month of fasting in the Muslim calendar.

shalwar kameez – Long, loose shirt and trousers worn by both men and women. A man's shalwar kameez is all one color, with pockets in the side and on the chest. A woman's shalwar kameez has different colors and patterns and is sometimes elaborately embroidered or beaded.

Red Crescent – The Muslim equivalent of the Red Cross, an international organization that provides aid to the sick and wounded in times of disaster and war.

Soviets – The Soviet Union before its break-up, including Russia and other Communist countries.

Taliban – An Afghan army that took control of the capital city of Kabul in September, 1996, and was forced from power in the fall of 2001.

toshak – A narrow mattress used in many Afghan homes instead of chairs or beds.

Deborah Ellis works as a counselor in a group home in Toronto. Her first children's book, *Looking for X*, won the Governor General's Award for Children's Literature. A few years ago Deborah traveled to Afghan refugee camps in Pakistan to interview women for her book of oral histories, *Women of the Afghan War*. The stories she heard and the children she met in those camps were also the inspiration for *The Breadwinner* and *Parvana's Journey*.